THE PASSING GRADE

TRISTAN R.B.

Copyright © 2012 Rio T. Charles Breakell (Tristan R.B.)

All rights reserved.

ISBN: 1481178261
ISBN-13: 978-1481178266

DEDICATION

I dedicate this novel to my late granddad, Chuck. He passed away when I was very young, but he had always been fully involved and dedicated to my writing, and was a huge fan of espionage novels and stories. Well, your love payed off... this one's for you.

Also dedicated to my mother, Sheila, as she was watching over my shoulder as I wrote this and guilted me into adding something about her.

You'll get 'em next book, Mom...

CONTENTS

Acknowledgments
And Forward

0	Prologue	1
1	Welcome To Camp	6
2	A Warm Greeting	19
3	The Plot Thickens	31
4	The Second Strike	43
5	Taking A Stand	56
6	Investigation	66
7	A Friend Falls	77
8	A Break For Peace	88
9	Slaughter	103
10	Silence Falls	122
11	Waiting, Dreading	133
12	The Killer Revealed	140
13	Aftermath	162
14	Epilogue	170

AUTHOR NAME

ACKNOWLEDGMENTS AND FORWARD

This book has had so many contributors... the unnamed book camp participant who turned me to the NANOWRIMO competition, my Mom and Dad for editing, my Friends and Family for putting up with my high strung attitude during the stressful month I wrote this, and the general attitude of encouragement that I received from everybody who knew of this competition. (Cheers Mr. Barnim)
Thank you.

This book should never have existed. I started my career as an author with the sequel, Order in Chaos, when I was nine. It started as a short story about a spy, and turned into an entire universe in my mind. I began rewriting Order in Chaos when I was fourteen, and halfway through I found out about the NANOWRIMO competition. I needed something short to write, and I decided upon going deeper into the background of the main character. Now, however, I can't see this series proceeding without some of the revelations held in these pages. So please, enjoy the story, that might not have been written...

PROLOGUE

Since an early age, Joshua Stone had not been a normal child. And people noticed. In fact, due to slightly enhanced cortical area in his brain, his entire life path had been shaped for him from minutes after he was born. A path through a dark and dangerous world, filled with terror, heartbreak, and violence. Orphaned at a young age, saved by a face he could not remember, and delivered to a tall, impersonal building. It was an orphanage for... spectacular orphans. He spent the next years of his life in a single facility, sunlight coming through windows too high to see out of. It was of a modern design, stainless steel and polished black appliances.

There were several other children in this orphanage, the number varied by the month. Few would join. The older ones would leave, some younger ones would leave. Josh always stayed. He would occasionally cross the hallway to enter the classrooms and training facilities. One man would always come to visit him, alongside the counselors and teachers that handled the facility. This man's name was Ace. Ace was tall, and muscular. He was young, but of course aged with Josh. He always wore a crisp, black suit with a blood red tie. He would tower over Josh, smiling down at him and telling him jokes and stories. These were very violent stories, but through the line of Josh's education, he was accustomed to violence.

Ace's physical condition would vary greatly between these visits. He would often be sporting a patched bullet hole, a casted arm, or a slight limp. One day he came to the orphanage in a wheelchair. Josh was amazed at finally being able to see eye to eye with this man. Through all this personal contact, he began to think of Ace as a father, a replacement for something he lost all too soon.

They studied the basic subjects, advanced theoretical math, AP sciences, English, Foreign Studies, Physical Education, History, Information Technology, and Geography. However, they also studied Martial Arts, Coding and Code Breaking, Stealth, Tactics, Weapon Disassembly/ Training, and Survival Skills.

Josh never really had any friends at the orphanage. He scared them. His slight hyper observance caused him to know everything they had done in the last forty eight hours, and what they were planning. This led to an especially embarrassing episode when Josh was at the age of sixteen, and involved a male and a female tenant of the orphanage. He became close friends with a boy named Mason. He was a massive hulk of a boy, muscles bulging over all 7'2" of him. Unfortunately, Mason was a full three years older than Josh, and had to leave the orphanage before him.

"Always eighteen. Why always eighteen?" Josh asked Ace, as they stood in the hallway, having just watched a group of four boys led away by three suited, sunglass clad guards. Ace examined Josh out of the corner of his eye. Josh now stood just shorter than Ace, dark stubble lined his jaw. A short scar ran down his right temple, a result of the training. Ace had watched this boy grow up, and now he was a man of sixteen.

"Because, Josh," Ace started. For some reason, standing there under the florescent lights, in the abandoned hallway, Ace felt closer to Josh than ever. He put his arm around Josh's shoulders, successfully suppressing tears, "Only then are they ready to face the horrors out there." Josh was closer than ever to Ace, but with his only friend gone, he felt lonelier than ever.

Two pages are too short to summarize such a long, tortured childhood of loss, physical, mental torment, and pain. I wish I had more time, but alas, the story must continue.

There came a time, one year later to the day, Josh was sitting in class, blindfolded, re-assembling an M4A1, when a tap of the door stirred movement in the room. Josh's ears twitched. He in his mind's eye he saw the disassembled gun in front of him, the parts on the table, the students around him, and the teacher making her way over to the door. The door opened and a heavy footstep moved into the room. He knew that weight, that step size.

"Ace!" He yelled, whipping off his blindfold and running toward the man. He had not seen Ace in three months, with no contact. Josh was worried that he had died. He hugged Ace, then took a step backward and examined the man. His tie was undone, sweat lined his brow, a distinct, slowly disappearing line around his mouth. Red on his hands. His hair was slightly messed. Mud on the shoes, fresh. A slight indentation on the nose, a bump on the left side of his right middle finger, a stressed look in his eye, he swallowed quickly.

"It's time, isn't it?" Josh asked. As always, Ace was taken aback by his skills of observation.

"How?" Ace asked.

"Obvious clues that you have been arguing or yelling with someone. Mud on your shoes, it was outside this facility, but not far. Your tie is undone. You never undo your tie. It was a long meeting. Your hair is messy, as if you had been running your hands through it. Indentation on your nose, reading glasses. The bump on the left side of the right side of your middle finger, you've been writing a lot. Final analysis... You've been arguing the terms of my early release, and signing the final paperwork. It was this day at this time that Mason left, and now it's my time. Also, you've been in Singapore for the last three months. For pleasure, not business," Josh replied, smirking as if it was obvious.

"Very... scary, Josh," Ace replied. He stepped aside and two guards in dark, ominous suits stepped through the door. Both wearing sunglasses. Josh looked back, all the other students were staring at him. He slowly made his way out into the hall, the two men followed him, lurking behind him, in case he tried to run. Ace came up alongside him, patting him on the shoulder.

"I can't bring anything, can I?" Josh asked. Ace shook his head. Josh nodded, making his way down the corridor, followed by Ace and the two men. As he drew nearer to the elevator, his sense of dread increased. He had always thought he would be glad to leave the orphanage, but he now realized that he had absolutely no idea what lay on the other side. No one who left ever came back. For all Josh knew, he could be taken into the elevator and shot in the head. He now realized why the guards were there. This realization almost made him want to run back. They came to the end of the hall, and Ace stopped. Josh turned, looking at him. A fresh cut ran along the man's left cheekbone.

"I can't take you any farther. The next steps you must take on your own," Ace said, in a calming voice. Josh was suddenly swept with turmoil, tears came to his eyes and a gasp to his throat. He launched himself forward at Ace, throwing his arms around the man's neck, hugging him tightly. Ace hugged him back. One of the guards cleared his throat. Ace pushed Josh off of him, wiping the tears from his eyes and stepped back. One of the guards laid a heavy hand on Josh's shoulder.

"Josh," Ace started, staring the man in the face, "You need to pay attention to me. Right now, what I'm saying to you is one of the most important pieces of information you will ever be given." Josh turned and looked at Ace, listening intently, "Don't trust anybody. Not even the instructors. Anybody can go mad in there, and who knows who already has. Josh, don't trust anybody. Your life... has been difficult. But it's about to get a lot harder, a lot more trying, a lot... scarier."

And with that the elevator chimed behind Josh. The two guards pulled him in. Just before the doors slid shut, Josh saw Ace smile and wave. It would be the last time Josh saw Ace, for a long while.

CHAPTER ONE

The dust billowed up around the back tires of the aged bus as it slowly pulled to a stop in front of the rickety, decrepit wooden building. The hot sun beat down on the sandy road as the glass doors of the bus swung open, and several weary, confused young men stepped out into the world, raising a hand to block out the rays. They stepped off the bus and marched toward the building, where two men in military dress stood by the open door. The air conditioning beckoned them.

"Hey, you in the back!" The bus driver yelled over his shoulder. The odd one in the back of the bus slowly stood up, cracking his neck after the long ride, slowly trudging his way down the aisle. "Don't let the boys in charge see you scrape your feet like that. Come on! On your toes!" The bus driver growled.

"You know what, thanks. Thanks a lot," Josh replied to the man, turning to step onto the road. The old man grunted in reply. Josh turned to examine the bright yellow and black school bus as the doors snapped shut, the engine revved, and a massive cloud of sand and dust shot up behind the vehicle as it pulled away. Josh slumped, the sun burning his eyes. The first time he had been outdoors in years, and he was dropped off in the middle of nowhere, not a tree in sight.

"Private! Up strait! 180 and march!" One of the guards yelled. Josh fixed his posture, spun on his heel and marched into the double doors, the cold air welcoming him. The doors slammed behind him. He was in a dimly lit room, filled with at least forty young men and women. Some chattered to each other, but most were silent. They all stood with impeccable posture, although Josh could not spot any guards in the room. Suddenly someone appeared on his right, a young man with fair hair and blue eyes.

"Hello there!" The perky young boy beamed at Josh.

"Um, hi," Josh replied, busy with internal reflection.

"The name's Spencer Eberstark! I'm here from new... er, I mean... I didn't come from any of the facilities, that is. Nope, my parents bought me in! I'm qualified, of course, but just not... selected, I guess? Anyway..." Spencer rambled on in a german accent.

"Oh, just shut up!" Josh suddenly snapped. Eberstark drew back slightly, obviously hurt.

"Listen, I'm sorry," Josh began, "But I've just left behind everything I've ever known, I'm the only one from my... facility, as you said... so, I just need a little time to myself."

"Oh, no worries! No worries at all!" Eberstark added, slipping away, "If you need me, I'll be... actually, I have no idea where I'll be. Hope we're in the same block!" Josh sighed. The chattering began to die down, everyone was facing the same way. Josh found this very odd. The crowd cringed back and shielded their eyes as a massive spotlight came upon them, from the front of the room. Josh's pupils shrunk to a nearly indistinguishable size.

"Attention!" A voice came over several loudspeakers. Josh recognized it as the voice of the guard from outside. "In a few moments, large doors in front of you will swing open. You will march through, take a sharp left, and enter the large brick building you find there. You will find your name on a plate on the ground. Stand behind it. Await further orders."

The speakers cut out and large doors opened, flooding the room with sunlight. The front row began to move, then the next, then the next. Finally Josh was moving forward, stepping once again out into the world, under the blistering sun.

The large brick building did not offer any air conditioning, and was excruciatingly hot. Josh found his name on the floor, it was near the door. He saw a man come up beside him. *You've gotta be kidding me!* Josh thought as Spencer Eberstark came up beside him, a large smile on his face.

"Hello again! Look at that! I did see you again!" The young man beamed. Josh rolled his eyes. Something caught his attention. He looked up to see a dozen shower heads positioned along the ceiling. As the large doors swung closed, thousands of images of nazis, genocide, gas drifting through the air, and dead bodies streamed through his head. Josh shook it off, sure Ace would not send him to his death. A man came through a small door in the wall, dressed in full military dress, complete with medals weighing down his left breast.

"Attention!" He called. All the young adults in the room straightened up, bringing their hands to their foreheads in salute. Josh followed suit. The man took a second to inspect the troops. "At ease," He called, and everyone dropped their hands, but remained rigid. Josh took a quick glance around. Everybody's eyes were riveted to the front of the room. He noted that there was a group of fifteen young women lined the back wall, while the remaining young men were in lines in front of them.

"Now!" The man at the front of the room called, "You may call me The General. I'm second in command here at Camp Razor's Edge, and I'm in charge of all of you. Now, this is not your orientation, this is your preparation stage. And I might as well tell you right now. Any insubordination toward staff, any disrespect toward me, my superior, or the two men ranking below me, will be met with serious consequences. You are free to settle any disputes between yourselves, however, murder will be met with serious consequences. Any sexual activity here at camp..."

"Let me guess, will be met with serious consequences," Spencer whispered to Josh, imitating The General's voice.

"You! Eberstark! Get up here!" The General called. Without blinking Spencer made his way up to the front of the room. Josh wanted to laugh, but avoided any break from formation at all costs.

"Yes, sir?" Spencer asked, standing at attention in the front of the room, directly in front of The General.

"Where are you from, boy?" The General asked.

"Germany, sir," Spencer replied.

"Alright. Strip!" The General yelled. After a second of disbelief, Spencer began to unbutton his shirt after a hard stare from The General. A few seconds later, he was standing naked but for his underwear, still straight as a board.

"All the way," The General continued. Spencer stood there for a second in shock. He then began to slowly remove his underwear. Soon he was naked.

"This is as much punishment as you will receive for talking out of turn. This time. This is the only warning, for all of you. Now, Eberstark, leave your clothes, return to your spot," The General called. Spencer turned on his heel, and returned to his spot next to Josh. There were a few seconds of silence. "Now," The General called, "The rest of you strip." There was a sudden burst of commotion through the room as men and women began to disrobe. "Fold your clothes in a neat manner, wrap them in your shirt or jacket, then pass them to the man on your left. The ones on the end, pile the clothing against the wall. Once you are done, stand at attention."

A few minutes later they were all naked, and the clothes were being collected by a guard with a large basket.

Josh felt awkward standing there naked, but the knowledge that everyone else had disrobed lightened the feeling.

"Ah yes, those clothes will make good fuel to cook your dinners on tonight!" The General called. A few gasps of shock rang out, but other than that, the crowd remained silent. A line of guards walked in, carrying each a razor. They positioned themselves on the end of each line, looking toward The General, who nodded. The guards switched the razors on, and began to move down the line, shaving every hair off of the troop's heads. The guard came to Josh. He felt the hairs fall over his body as the razor ran over his scalp, massaging it. The guard moved on to the next man. Josh's hand immediately moved to his head. They had left no hair behind, not even fuzz. The skin he had never felt before felt very strange under his fingers. He looked to Spencer, his head seemed oversized without its hair. Josh assumed he must have looked something the same. Suddenly there was a hiss of water, and freezing liquid cascaded down from the ceiling, splashing down on the troops, several shrieks pierced the air. Josh clenched his fists and jaw, the cold water felt scalding, in high contrast to the blistering sun he had experienced outside the facility.

"Wash yourselves. You have five minutes of water," The General called out. Josh immediately began to wash himself, assuming he would not have another shower for a long time. After several minutes of cold torture, the water shut off, leaving the room full of young adults shivering and clutching at themselves. The General smirked, enjoying their discomfort. The large doors opened again, and a line of guards entered, carrying rough towels. Josh was handed a heavy stack. He took one of the course pieces of material, then handed the stack down the line. As he dried himself his skin turned red from the burn of the towel. He wrapped the towel around his waist, the water on the floor draining slowly.

The guards came by again, dropping a brown paper package at the foot of each man, their name written on it in dark black sharpie. Josh eyed the package. Images of scorched ground, burnt bodies, and wires filed through his mind.

"Open your packages!" The General called. Josh leaned down and ripped the paper open. Digitized camouflage material met his eyes. "These are your action and formal dress. You will wear these for any formal meeting, and any testing that occurs. When you arrive at your living quarters, you will find your casual clothes and other items in a chest. When the doors open, we will direct you to your blocks. You will have one hour to socialize with the other troops in your block, before the formal orientation. You will attend in these clothes. Now, get dressed."

As Josh pulled the course fabric over his shivering body, he shuddered at the thought of not having a change of clothes waiting for him. He leaned down to tie the laces of the thick black military boots. He pulled the ACU cap over his shaved head, and slipped on the black tactical gloves. He looked around. Other than the looks in their eyes, the individuality had been completely wiped from these men and women... this personalities hammered and formed by the machine, made into one. Suddenly Josh's thoughts were interrupted as Spencer tapped him on the shoulder.

"There's something left in your pack.The guards are coming to collect them. Better get it fast," He whispered into Josh's ear. Josh glanced up, seeing two men wearing sunglasses and wielding AK-94u's strutting down the line ahead of them. Josh quickly bent down again, pushing aside the material to reveal a small brown paper package. An elegant A in sweeping handwriting sprawled across the package. Josh's mood lightened significantly. Ace had come through for him, once again. The guards were coming. Assuming the package was contraband, he stuffed it in the pocket of the jacket. The guards came by, grabbed the packaging materials, and continued walking. Josh let out his breath.

Minutes later the line began to move. The boots made a hellish noise on the tiles as the men strode across the threshold, out the door and into the yard. As Josh stepped out the door he came face to face with a man in official military dress. He looked at Josh, looked down at a sheet, then looked back up.

"Block C," The man yelled suddenly, pointing to his left. Josh turned on his heel, making his way toward a large steel building with a huge orange C on the side. It resembled a military aircraft hanger. He glanced back. To his displeasure he saw Spencer bouncing along behind him, beaming.

"Block C, the both of us! Can you believe that? What luck, the first friendly person I've met here, and we're in the same block! Thats just fantastic! I mean, who has smiled upon me to-" Spencer rattled on as he quickened his pace to catch up to Josh.

"Spencer," Josh muttered.

"Yeah?"

"Shut up, Spencer,"

"I got ya. No need to apologize for ye-"

"Shut up, Spencer," Josh repeated. This time Spencer just nodded. The two came into the shadow of the large building, the sun cut out it became very cold. Josh saw a man standing in the massive doorway, a clipboard in his hand.

"Names?" The man asked.

"Joshua Stone," He answered. There was a long pause. Spencer was tapping Josh's elbow, as if requesting to speak. Josh turned on him, glaring.

"My name's Spencer Eberstark," Spencer answered, not looking away from Josh's deathly eyes.

"Josh, you're down in section D, fifth bed. Spencer, Section A, ninth bed," The man said after a while. Josh turned away from Spencer, disappearing into the building. Spencer followed behind him. They were met by a massive space, filled with lines of bunks, some men in military garb wandered around, exploring the chests at the foot of their beds, or entering the steel cube in the center of the room, most likely the restrooms and showers. Spencer took a hard left, entering a painted off area with a large A along the walkway. Josh spotted a D further down the hall. He walked up and took a left, finding bunk five. He fell onto the bed. He was met by a rock hard mattress dressed with wire thin olive green sheets.

    He let the package fall from his jacket. He ripped open the paper, spreading the contents about the bed. There was two thousand dollars in Canadian twenty dollar bills, a pair of sunglasses, a roll of duct tape, a notebook and a pen, a box of matches, and to top it all off a Colt Anaconda seven round revolver. Josh gripped the weapon in his palm, feeling the weight, stroking the trigger. He flicked out the roll and spun it. It glided smoothly.

    "Wow, is that even allowed?" A voice asked from somewhere, Josh quickly spun to see a pair of eyes and a forehead hanging down from the bunk above Josh. The man quickly pulled his head back up, not enjoying staring down the barrel of the silver weapon. Suddenly the man fell from the bunk above him, landing in a crouching position, at eye level with Josh. "I like illegal things. I think that the thrill is fun. Not much of a pistol guy personally, I like snipers. I love watching people freak out when the guy standing next to them falls in a puddle of blood before they even hear the gunshot."

    "What's your name?" Josh asked, slightly lowering his revolver.

    "Alex. I'll see if I can trust you before I can tell you my last name," Alex stood up, running his forefinger across his forehead a, a habit of those with long bangs. Of course, he had lost his bangs. He lowered his hand awkwardly, then puffed out his chest to compensate for the loss of image.

    "The name's Josh. I'll tell you my last name when-"

"Stone! Joshua Stone!" Eberstark yelled, running down the hall. He came to Josh's bunk, panting and out of breath.

"Shit," Josh whispered, the air of mystery gone.

"The General's looking for you," Spencer panted heavily. His eyes bugged when he spotted the gun in Josh's hand. Josh slid it in his pocket, slipped off his jacket and laid it over the other items on the bed. He stood up and followed Spencer away. He turned back quickly. Nobody was there, but he knew that Alex was following them. They came to the door of the building, where The General and ten guards stood. Josh swallowed. Did they know about the package?

"Joshua Stone?" The General asked. Josh nodded, "So you're the recruit from HQ. Very interesting. You know, last year we had three from HQ, one of them was freakishly tall..."

"Mason!" Josh exclaimed.

"Yes, that was his name. I can see you two were friends, I'm glad to inform you that he survived, and passed. He's positioned in Monaco as we speak," The General informed Josh. Josh's face lit up, excited by the news of his old friend.

"Surely that's not the only reason you've called me here," As the words left Josh's mouth he realized what a mistake it was. Ten steps away, behind a brick wall, Alex cringed. The General glared Josh down coldly.

"The reason I have called you here is because your file says that you are 'Extremely Gifted'. Here at Razor's Edge, we don't like that. It's the ones like you, who think they're good at something, and because of that do whatever the hell they want. I think it comes from my brother's carefree mentoring style." Then suddenly Josh saw it. The jawline, the eyes, the nose... he was talking to Ace's brother. Could he have been the one that sent the package? No... *He's too strict.* "Basically," The General continued, "I'm here to tell you to stay out of trouble. At all costs."

"Thank you, Sir!" Josh exclaimed, snapping to attention. The General nodded then spun on his heel, as he walked away the guards followed suit. Josh relaxed his stance as Alex swept around the corner.

"You're from HQ?" He asked Josh.

"I don't really know what that means," Josh replied.

"It means you've got the best chance of surviving this hell hole over all of us. Wow, now I see why someone wanted so desperately to get you that gun," Alex whispered to Josh as they strode through Block C, not wanting anybody to overhear.

"Why? If I have the best chances of surviving, why would I be the one who needs the gun?" Josh whispered back.

"Because your in the most danger from the rest of *us*. People out there hear your from HQ, they'll kill you for your money, which they will know you have, or for your food, because you'll be getting better rations, or just to eliminated from the equation... you know only the top ten percent get out of here as an agent," Alex whispered back in a rushed tone, his mouth barely moving. Josh assumed many people had been trained to read lips, as he had.

"How do you know all of this? I just arrived here, all I know is that its a death camp!" Josh exclaimed as they came to their bunks, falling to a sitting position on Josh's bed.

"The other places these guys come from aren't as intense as HQ. We still had lives, etc, and knew about this place long before we came here," Alex replied, slipping the revolver from Josh's pocket, admiring his skill, Josh having not noticed. Josh looked to his left.

"Hey, give that back," Josh barked, snapping it from Alex's hands, slipping it back into his pocket.

"There's a black market that goes on here between guards and us guys. Thats why you got that cash. Here's a suggestion. The first thing you want to buy is a coding device, get two in fact. They'll come in handy. Also, you should buy a guard. He'll vouch for you if you get caught doing anything," Alex explained, jumping up onto his bed. Josh whipped the jacket off his bed and slid it on, stuffing the items into his pockets. He went around to the foot of his bed, and flung open the trunk.

It contained a black and red sling pack, a folded set of black, waterproofed pants, a grey and black t shirt, and a black jacket to top it all off. The material was soft, Josh was beaming at the thought of changing into them later. There was also a set of pajamas, as well as several pairs of socks and underwear. The trunk also contained a large, clear bag of toiletries, a towel, a plate and spoon, a cup, a pair of running shoes, and a roll of toilet paper. Josh replaced the items in the chest, just as Spencer came running back up the aisle.

"The... meeting... thing..... starts... in two minutes. Long.... walk.... must leave.... now," Eberstark panted to Josh. Josh relayed the info to Alex, who again jumped to the ground, landing like a cat. He stood up, straightened his jacket, then followed Josh and Spencer out of the building. The sun had begun to set, so the scorching heat let up a little, allowing the three men to sprint. After a minute they came to the large gathering building in the center of the yard. They kicked through the large double doors, filing into the large atrium, the rows and rows of young men in military dress chatted with each other, a massive cataclysm of noise echoing off the walls.

Josh, Alex and Spencer found seats in the middle of the stands, next to two men talking about a football game. The lights came down and a spotlight hit the stage. The crowd fell so silent Josh could hear the doors lock. He thought of how easy it would be for somebody to burn the place down, *killing us all*. The General stepped onto the stage, approached the podium, and tapped the microphone.

"Attention troops! All stand for the entrance of The Master!" The General stepped to the side and saluted as the young men and women stood at attention, sweat dripping down their brows. There were no windows in the building. A man in red, silken military dress came from doors behind the stage, a long flowing cape followed behind him. Twenty guards followed. They were not the same as the others, their chests shone with many metals, and they wore full metal face masks. Swords hung from their hips. The Master came up to the mic, and the guards lined the stage behind him. Regular guards lined in front of the stage, rifles aimed into the crowd.

"Hello, troops of Camp's Razor's Edge. In this camp, some of you will die. This is a fact," The Master began. His voice was mesmerizing. The rest of the orientation was boring, mostly facts about life at camp, and ended when the soldiers, that is what the men were called now, filed out of the building, the guards wiping red paint across their foreheads. Back in Block C, Josh stared at the bottom of the bunk above him. He could not sleep. His life had changed so much in one day. The pajamas were comfortable, but the sheets were far too hot. They were drenched in sweat already, but if Josh swept them aside he was immediately assaulted by mosquitoes.

"Are you asleep?" Josh whispered, tapping the bottom of Alex's bed.

"No," Came the faint reply.

"Are you boiling?"

"Are you kidding me? I'm from England! This is bloody ridiculous!"

"What do you think we are going to do tomorrow?" Josh asked. There was no reply. "Hello?" Josh asked. Suddenly he noticed that a shadow had passed in front of the window. One of the night guards, armed with a fully automatic rifle. "Alex?" Josh asked. Suddenly there was a massive bang on the wall.

"Quiet in there!" The guard yelled. The shadow continued on.

"Josh?" Alex asked.

"Yeah?" Josh whispered back.

"I just realized that they never gave us dinner."

CHAPTER TWO

Joshua Stone ran for his life, the sweat dripping down his brow. The heavy gun began to slip in his hands, the grip slicked by perspiration. He heard Spencer panting along behind him. The thick branches smashed into his face, catching on his tactical vest, ripping at his exposed forearms. He could hear gunfire in the distance, and from close behind them. He heard a call from his partner. He turned to see Spencer laying on the ground, his foot stuck in a twisted root. Josh spun and dove to his knees, examining the error. Spencer writhed on the ground, yelling at Josh to continue without him.

"Leave no man behind," Josh breathed, hacking at the branch with the large military knife. He heard the bushes moving close behind them. He grabbed Spencer by the shoulders, beginning to pull him out of his boots.

"Come on Eberstark! Fight for it!" Josh yelled. The foot finally slid out of the boot. Josh dragged Spencer into the bushes off the side of the path. He heard shots fired, and the projectiles whizzed by their heads and shoulders. The team they had been stalking was a marksman group, they obviously had not seen Josh yet, or he would be dead. Spencer's foot disappeared into the thick bush just as the team of five men arrived at the root. One bent down to examine the boot.

"This is a C Block boot," The man told his team mates. Josh held his breath, and his hand was firmly over Spencer's mouth, he could feel him twitching with fear. Dirty sweat streamed over his brow. His fatigues were covered in mud. For the first time it occurred to Josh that there may be no way to wash them.

"Look at these marks. It looks like somebody has been dragged into the bush," Another voice called. Josh's heart rate quickened. They were going to be found. A fly buzzed around Josh's face. It landed on his nose. Josh had to sneeze.

"Nobody would be stupid enough to leave a boot behind and hide in the bush directly next to it. It must be a trap. We'll scout ahead. Samir, check that bush for a claymore." The first man ordered.

"Copy," The one named Samir replied. The rest of the group moved ahead while the man named Samir moved toward the bush. Josh took his hand off of Spencer's mouth, who nodded at Josh. Josh slowly got to his feet, gently brushing bushes away so as to remain silent. Samir broke through the foliage, scanning the ground. Josh was upon him. He wrapped his arm around the mans mouth, slipping the knife from it's sheath and bringing it up the the man's neck.

"If you struggle, I'll slit your throat," Josh growled quietly. The man nodded. "Where is Block A's weapon cache located?" Josh demanded. He slowly removed his hand from the man's mouth.

"Center of the field, hidden in the bush next to the large cedar tree," The man whimpered.

"Thanks. Now listen, I'm not going to kill you. I'm going to leave you here. In two minutes, you will leave this bush and walk back to your home base. You will report that you got separated from your unit. Nothing else. If you move from this spot, I have a sniper that will kill you. Thanks for your help," Josh explained, releasing the man. Spencer stood up, they retrieved his boot and they ran down the path, following Samir's team. Josh pulled his rifle off his back, swinging it around to his hip. The enemy team came into view. Josh and Spencer dropped to the ground as one, slowly crawling closer. There were four of them. Josh turned to look at Spencer.

"I'll shoot far left, you take far right. Then I will hit left center, then you take out right center. If you miss the first shot, move to the second. Then go back to the first. Make sure they are both hit before you move up. Safety off. On my mark," Josh whispered. They were ten meters out.

"What's the mark?" Spencer whispered back.

"You'll know it," Josh replied. The team had begun moving forward again, lined across the path. Josh took his aim, held his breath, then kicked Spencer.

BANG BANG BANG BANG. The four men fell. Josh scrambled to his feet, Spencer on his tail. They came up to the men. Josh felt their pulse. Josh grabbed a man by the arm and dragged him to the bush, then the second man. They kicked dirt across the drag marks. Josh slung his rifle against his back and continued down the path. Spencer followed him. He clicked the radio on his shoulder, the thing buzzed to life.

"Block C report. How many lost?" Josh asked.

"We've lost half the team, Josh. Block B is completely wiped, D is holding on with three men, E is wiped, and A is holding strong with three quarters remaining," A voice replied.

"Copy that. Mark off six more A's. And I know where their weapon's cache is. Center of the field, in the bush next to the Cedar," Josh barked into the radio.

"Good to know," The voice came back over the speaker.

"Is Alex still in?" Josh asked.

"Yeah, I'm here," The voice patched in. Josh let out his breath. Josh and Spencer came into a large clearing. They crouched, slowly moving forward, rifles raised. They were expecting an ambush. They were right. Suddenly gunfire exploded into the clearing behind them. Spencer rolled to his right, Josh dove to his left. The dirt where they had been seconds before exploded. Josh found himself laying behind a log. He looked up and saw two men emerging from the bush in front of him. The fire continued from behind, Josh snapped up his rifle and shot the two, they rag-dolled to the mud.

The bullets flying from behind Josh ceased. He peaked around the log, firing three shots, taking out two men. He glanced over to see Spencer laying on a slight incline, a rip on his shoulder marked a near miss. Bullets flew by Josh's head, stripping wood off the log. Josh pulled his head back in. He tore at his tactical vest, a grenade falling into his hand. He ripped the pin out with his mouth, holding in the safety release. He pulled a mirror out of his pocket, he wanted to watch this.

He released the safety, waited three seconds, then hurled the grenade over his head. He lifted the mirror. He saw the three men stop firing, panicking. One swooped down and picked up the grenade, preparing to throw it back. The small sphere exploded in his hand, spreading green smoke over the area. The three men dropped, Josh scrambled out and grabbed Spencer by the arm, pulling him to his feet.

"Don't breath that!" Josh yelled, pulling Spencer along as they ran from the place. Josh guided Spencer through the bush, sprinting in fear of reinforcements finding the bodies. It began to rain. Somehow, this God damned place could stay ridiculously hot while also sending tiny bullets showering from the sky, leaving long red streaks across Josh's face. They slowed down, catching their breath, panting, sweat mixing with the rain. Josh sat on a large, twisted root, pulling Spencer down beside him. They began laughing. They didn't know why, or at what. But something in that dark forest was so hilarious that they laughed heartily.

Then Josh stopped laughing. He grabbed at his back. There was no rifle slung there. He had left it, in the clearing with the toxic gas. He could not return for it. He pulled the pistol from his leg, checking the ammunition.

"Come in, Stone! Eberstark? Do you read me?" A voice buzzed over the radio.

"Joshua Stone, reporting in," Josh voiced into the mic.

"There's only thirty others left from C Block.... A Block is still going strong with thirty percent... God, this has been some battle. I don't know where you are, but you need to get to center field. We destroyed their weapons cache... It was a fake. My team was hit with snipers, and infantry units flooded the hills. The rest of C Block is here, we need you Josh! Get over here!" Josh's pulse quickened. His team needed him, and there was no force on earth that could stop him from getting to center field. He ripped the water-proofed map from his chest, spreading it out on the log. He took a red sharpie and circled the center field. After he triangulated their current position, he marked where snipers were most likely positioned.

"Lets move," He yelled at Spencer, jumping to his feet and sprinting north through the bush. After five straight minutes of bush whacking, Josh suddenly dropped to his knees. He pulled Spencer down with him, clapping a hand over his mouth. He put a curled finger up to his eye, wrapped his hand around his wrist, then pointed at the ridge. Spencer nodded. Enemy sniper on the ridge. Josh slowly moved forward, cocking his pistol. They emerged from the trees. The sounds of gunfire and screams met them. A thin layer of fog clouded the air. Josh scanned the small grassy plato, spotting the ghillie suited sniper laying in the center, peering down the scope of a long, black rifle.

Josh slowly moved upon him, pistol aimed, holding his breath as he moved forward. He knew at any moment a sniper on one of the surrounding hills could spot him and take him out. As he drew closer to the edge, the valley below came into view. Bodies everywhere. Bullets flew through the air, the C Block boys cowering behind various fallen trees and overturned tables in the center of the clearing, the infantry from Block A about the edges of the clearing, not even bothering to take cover. It was a massacre.

Josh was upon the sniper. He put the pistol to the man's head, who jumped at the feeling of the cold steel.

"Hand over your rifle, and your radio," Josh demanded. The sniper followed the orders, Josh slung the rifle about his back, and clipped the radio to his belt. He then shot the sniper in the head. *No risks*. He lay in the same position the man had, putting his eye to the cold scope. He adjusted the crosshairs, centering them on a man down in the clearing, who was attempting to sneak around behind the C Block line. Josh squeezed the trigger. The gun let of a loud BANG and two seconds later he watched the man drop.

Josh pulled back the bolt, loading another shot into the weapon. He scoped again, shot, and watched a man drop. Suddenly the enemy's radio blared to life.

"C Block has a sniper on our position! Take 'em out!" The radio demanded. Josh's first though was of Alex, then he realized that they were talking about him. He pressed himself into the ground, standing up was a death sentence.

"Josh, you stupid, glorious bastard!" A voice came over the C Block radio. It was Alex's voice.

"Eh?" Josh grunted.

"You've given me free license to take all of these morons out while they're looking at you!" Josh glanced up to see men falling quickly in the clearing. A bullet flew by his head, he dropped it again.

"Focus on taking out the enemy snipers so that I can get back in the game!" Josh yelled into the radio.

"Copy," Alex replied. Josh pressed his body further into the dirt, sweat pouring off his brow, adrenaline raging as projectiles whizzed past him, millimeters from his head, he could feel their speed on his scalp. He had never felt more alive. Suddenly, there was a cease fire. Josh slowly looked up. He cautiously put the sniper rifle to his eye, and continued taking out A Block soldiers.

Click. Josh dropped the gun and stood up, taking the pistol from the snipers body, readying his own, then edged closer to the drop from the ridge. Spencer came up behind him.

"I don't think I can make it down there," He whimpered.

"Then wait here," Josh barked, grabbing Spencer's rifle then sliding off the edge. The earth whipped by him as he flew down the side of the unbelievably steep slope, grinding down the soles of his boots. All too soon he was on flat ground. He rolled, coming to his feet behind a stack of overturned barrels. He snapped out to his right, bringing his weapon up and quickly firing off two shots, taking down a man running across the field. He came back behind the barrels as bullets ricocheted off the cylinders, the sound of metal on metal resoundingly deafening. Josh quickly swung around the left side of the barrels, squeezing off three rounds, taking out two men before the bullets reached him.

Josh dropped down to his chest, slowly crawled along the ground away from the oil drums. The long grass disguised him well, but he was afraid of somebody seeing the grass rustle. He came up to a large boulder and slowly slid up to his feet, hugging the stone. His put his gun to his shoulder, swung around the boulder, and ran, spraying toward the enemy. His vision blurred white with adrenaline, the small bits of metal spraying past him, the air ripping at his skin, the gun shaking in his hands. He dove back behind the barrels, the end of his weapon smoking. He dropped the mag and slid in another from his belt, pulling back the hammer.

"Its useless! There's too many of them!" Somebody yelled from Josh's right. He recognized it as a member of C Block. It was true, the A Block forces were pushing forward, and they were outnumbered four to one. Josh slid to a sitting position on the ground, almost accepting defeat. Then there was a humming far away. Josh dismissed it. The noise grew louder... louder... Josh recognized it. And the tide of war changed.

    The helicopter roared over the cliff, unleashing a massive mounted gun upon the crowd, members of C Block falling all over the ground. Josh saw a man strapped to the side of the helicopter, taking quick shots from a long rifle.

    "Alex you fabulous son of a bitch!" Josh yelled into his mic.

    "Me and two buddies found this old boy under a ghillie tarp. We were in the air seconds later!" The reply came over the radio.

    "Retreat! Pull back into the forest! We don't stand a-*GRAG!*" A voice blared over the C Block radio on Josh's belt. The man had died. Josh discarded the radio. The helicopter hovered in the air, unloading onto the enemies below. Josh stood up, watching the spectacle, men shot down as they ran from the flying metal beast. Josh ran out into the open, firing upon the crowd. His teammates followed suit, stepping out and moving forward. Josh chased the men into the bush, followed by his teammates and the helicopter. As he ran through the bush, dodging branched and jumping logs, the powerful wind of the chopper beating down on him, he couldn't help thinking of the tapes of Vietnam, the blood on the screen... And to add insult to injury, Fortunate Son by CCR cracked to life from a speaker somewhere in the helicopter.

    The C Block team came into a clearing, the helicopter began to land. The grass was crushed flat, Alex jumped to the ground before the vehicle touched down. He ran up to Josh, throwing his arms around him, embracing him in a tight hug.

    "You won't believe the shit I've seen out there today!" Alex exclaimed.

    "Its almost like a real war!" Josh yelled back, holding his friend out to examine him. Spencer ran up to them from nowhere, clapping a hand on each's shoulders.

    "Eberstark!" Alex yelled.

"I'm actually glad to see you!" Josh called. The three men burst into happy tears, shocked that they had survived the last ordeal. Josh looked around at the men amassed in the clearing. A troubled look crossed his face. He climbed atop the chopper, raised his hands, and yelled at the men, who immediately fell silent.

"Attention! Is the Captain still alive?" Josh yelled. There were negative statements, "Alright then. Remember, this game isn't over until one block remains. We will split up and hunt down the rest of that damned A Block!" This arose cheers, "But we are extremely outnumbered. We are going guerrilla from here on out. Stick to groups of at least two, no more than four. Keep to the shadows. Only shoot what you can kill. Take on large numbers of enemies with the element of surprise. And no matter what happens, remember the faces you see here today, because even if we all get killed, we have won, for we have made it this far."

And that was how Josh won the respect of his Block. A loud cheer rang out "Josh! Josh! Josh!" Josh jumped down from the chopper as the men grouped up and dispersed. He grabbed two men.

"You operate radio?" Josh asked one.

"Yes," The man replied.

"Can you pilot a chopper?" Josh asked the other.

"Like I can walk," The other answered.

"You two take the chopper high, and radio out the enemy positions. There may be other large weapons hidden out here, so watch for missiles. Go!" Josh yelled.

"Sir!" The two yelled, jumping into the chopper. Josh signaled Alex and Spencer to follow him.

*

*

*

Hours later, sweat pouring down his brow, Josh sat on a stump. The sun had begun to set, they had run out of water two hours ago, and the climate only got hotter. The reports said that there were only three members of A Block left, and they were playing it well, leaving groups as large as ten dead in their path. The chopper had run out of gas a long time ago, so they had no idea where the enemy was. Josh stood up, kicking Spencer awake and calling Alex down from the tree. Alex jumped to another branch, swung down, ran along the branch then jumped to the ground.

"We need to move. If the sun sets and they aren't dead, rules say no rations tomorrow. And I need meat, boys," The three men hacked their way through the bush, swatting away bugs as they made their way through the bush. Josh took the lead, the other two followed in a row behind him. Minutes later, they came to a partial clearing. Five minutes to sunset. Suddenly Josh heard a whooshing sound behind him.

He spun, raising his gun. Two figures dressed in tight black fatigues crouched above the crumpled bodies of Spencer and Alex. The two had dropped from the trees, taking the boys out with knives. Josh rolled to his left as a third dropped, jumping to their feet, their knife impaled on the ground. Josh brought up his rifle and took out the two that had killed Alex and Spencer, and dove to avoid a slice from the blade of the third attacker. Josh got a good look that time.

Black plastic-like suit, skin tight, obviously designed for stealth and free running. There was a mask over the face and head, looked like part of the suit... the curve at the chest indicated.... *a woman?*

"There are no members of Block E Left!" Josh exclaimed.

"I know that. Me and my girls, the ones you just killed, thought it would be more strategic to sell our strengths to the obviously superior block," The feminine voice called from behind the dark mask. Josh dodged another blow, but the woman's other hand twisted the rifle from his hands. He rolled to his left, coming up on his feet. The two slowly circled each other. Josh thought of his options. Either he killed this woman, or got killed. It was as simple as that. He was disgusted by the fact that these three women had sold out their own block just to have a better chance at winning. He pulled a knife from his vest.

Suddenly there was movement, the woman lunged forward, Josh side stepped the attack, bringing his hand down on her arm, knocking the knife from her grip. She dove to the ground, rolling, coming up armed again. Josh came forward, throwing a punch at her stomach. At the last second he redirected the punch, but she had expected it. A leg came up and violently kicked Josh backward, who stumbled into a tree. The woman ran at him, he rolled to the side to avoid the attack.

Josh slid around the side of the tree, dashed around again and was met with a fist. He sprawled on the dirt, the masked woman towering over him. They thought exactly the same, each move was mirrored, each thought repeated... this was an interesting fight. Josh flipped up to his feet, readying himself for another onslaught. She sprinted up, tossing a punch at Josh's throat. Josh spun to the side, grabbing her arm and twisting, flipping her to the ground. Josh placed a foot atop her forehead, keeping her down. Then something surprising happened. She flipped to her feet, which would have caused excruciating pain in her forehead. She was a fighter.

Josh sidestepped a few attacks, launched a few of his own, it was a never ending fight. Finally she made a mistake. The woman ran at Josh, Josh sidestepped, sticking out a leg. The woman toppled to the ground, and took slightly too long to stand. Josh was on top of her, pinning her to the ground, slowly pulling the pistol from her thigh. He placed the barrel on her forehead.

"Good fight," He panted.

"Thanks," She replied. Josh suddenly had an urge to know who he had been locked in mortal combat with this whole time. He whipped off the mask. Long, flowing brown hair tumbled out, masking soft, beautiful features. Josh was taken aback. And that was his mistake. The woman rolled, taking Josh with her. She was now above him, the pistol in her hand.

"Nice try, but like all men, you have your weaknesses. Better luck next time," She panted, pressing the barrel into Josh's forehead. Josh took and held a deep breath, squeezing his eyes shut.

"Oh, that's low..." He whispered. The woman pulled the trigger. Josh felt a sharp, burning pain in his forehead, Everything went black, then he stopped thinking.

CHAPTER THREE

Josh slowly woke up, a bright white light straining through his shut eyelids, he felt a course bandage wrapped around his forehead, it was wet. He was warm, under heavy sheets. There were various noises around him, but none he could pick out individually. He slowly opened his eyes, sensitive to the light.

"He's awake!" A familiar voice called from somewhere to his left. Alex rushed up to Josh, shaking him awake. Josh's eyes flew open, Alex was standing there in muddy battle fatigues, a bandage around his neck.

"Those tranquilizer rounds sure pack a punch, eh Josh?" Alex asked.

"Hell yeah, I'm just glad I wasn't one of the guy's hit by the helicopter!" Josh laughed, standing up from the bed. He ripped the bandage off of his head, it was covered in a light layer of blood. He looked down, he was still covered in mud and dirt, he was bruised and cut, and probably looked like hammered shit.

"What time is it?" Spencer asked from behind Josh. Josh spun to look at his friend. He also had a bandage around his neck, and a long cut ran along the left side of his face. He was also still covered in mud.

"Six o'clock," Alex answered.

"Still in time for dinner!" Josh bounced giddily.

"Nope, there was still one member of C Block left, no food tonight or tomorrow," Alex corrected.

"Damn it!" Josh cursed, kicking the bed, "I could have killed her."

"Her?"

"Three women sold themselves out to A Block as assassins, they're the ones that took you out," Josh replied.

"Bitches!" Alex exclaimed.

"More like strategic," A voice called from behind. The three men turned to see three woman, in skintight black battle suits. Josh recognized the one in front as the woman who had "killed" him, her brown hair tied back. The other two women, both with blond hair, must have been the ones that dropped from the trees and killed Spencer and Alex.

"Hello again," Josh called, smirking.

"Surprised to see you guys awake so quick, that was heavy stuff we hit you with," She smirked back. The woman stopped about three feet from the men, both groups examining each other. They stood there for some sixty seconds, just examining, measuring, and taking in each other.

"Well, let me introduce myself," Josh announced, "The name's Joshua Stone."

"Stone? That's a little... cliché, isn't it?" The girl retorted.

"You leave him alone! Um... by the way, my name's Spencer Eberstark. I'm from Germany. My parents bought my way into this camp, but I'm still pretty good. I'm not that rich myself but-"

"Spencer, shut up," Alex smacked him lightly, "I'm Alex, just... Alex." Alex extended his hand to the blonde on the right, obviously flirting with her. It was odd, Josh thought, he had also thought of that woman as a potential partner.

"Okay... My name's Alexis. I've been elected leader of E Block, so just stay out of my way," The brunette that had shot Josh said, still smirking.

"I'm Julia, Alexis's sister," The blonde on the left said.

"And my name is Mizuki Kimura," The blonde that Josh and Alex had taken fancy to said, "My parents are Japanese, and they adopted me very young, I took their last name, but as you can see, I'm not japanese myself." She beamed, chuckling. The three women turned and walked off, laughing to each other, leaving the three men perplexed.

Minutes later Josh was back at his bunk, he had changed into his casual clothes, and was writing in the journal about the horrors he had seen out on the battlefield. Alex lay above him, playing with Josh's revolver. Josh could hear the metal clicking and twisting, Josh assumed that by now Alex had taken the entire gun apart, put it back together, then repeated it.

"Josh, you want to hit the showers? No point staying in clean clothes anymore if I've got dirt down to my toes!" Alex called from the bunk. Josh agreed with him. He snapped the book shut and stood up, stretching his back. He slowly made his way to the showers, feeling the weight of the toiletries bag. Alex fell in step behind him. Josh pulled open the heavy metal door, hit by warm, moist steam. He peeled off his clothes, shoving them into a cubby by the door. He found an empty spot, and flipped the switch. A mistake. The freezing water came down on him, he jumped and screeched. He looked up to see Alex standing beside a stream of water, laughing at Josh.

Josh felt the temperature raise, and stepped back into the shower. He pulled the shampoo from the bag, lathering his bald scalp and washing the dirt and grime off the rest of his body. He also took the time to brush his teeth, seeing as there would be no dinner. Josh suddenly heard the shower doors burst open, and saw Spencer run in, fully dressed.

"Every time you need me, how do you seem to find me?" Josh asked.

"Intuition," Spencer replied, "I just wanted to know if you knew that there was a full camp meeting tonight."

"I know you know I know," Josh replied.

"What?" Spencer asked.

"Alex, explain," Josh smirked.

"Well, all I know is that I know you know that he knows you know, and by the way I do know," Alex called from behind shampoo covered eyes.

"I'm still confused," Spencer raged.

"Its simple!" Josh began, "I know that Alex knows that I know that you know I know, Alex knows, and although you may not know we all collectively know. You know?"

"No!" Spencer replied, "You know that he knows that I know that- You know what? Just show up to the meeting tonight! Half an hour. God you guys, sometimes...." Spencer muttered to himself as he exited the room.

"You think he would have known!" Josh exclaimed. This arose a massive, roaring laugh from Alex. Josh shut off the water, enjoying the sauna like environment. He slowly made his way over to the doors, drying himself off before pulling his clothes on. He exited the room to hear cacophonous cheers and shouts from the back of the building. Josh ran to see what the disturbance was. He pushed through the crowd amassed by the back wall, coming to the front of the semicircle to see two men slowly circling each other, hate in their eyes. Josh was shocked to realize that one of the combatants was Spencer.

"Eberstark! What the hell are you doing?" Josh yelled. Spencer seemed not to hear him. His left eye was bruised and blood dripped from his nose. Suddenly the stranger dashed forward, Spencer sidestepped it, throwing a hand into the enemy's back, he sprawled to the floor. Spencer readied an offensive position as the stranger flipped back to his feet. The enemy came at Spencer again, a fist aimed for his throat.

"Spencer look out!" Josh yelled, he had seen the feint before. As Spencer reached to to grab the man's hand, the enemy reached up with his other arm and took hold of Spencer's wrist. Spencer threw a punch at the man, but the enemy caught Spencer's other wrist. Spencer looked down to realize that the man was standing on his feet. With a light shove, Spencer was sent to the ground, landing hard on his back. The man descended on him, throwing punches at his face, over and over again, blood spraying up.

Josh couldn't contain himself anymore. He stepped out into the ring, grabbing the man by the back and pulled him off Spencer, throwing him to the other side of the space.

"What's your name?" Josh asked the man.

"Why do you want to know?"

"So that I know who I'm beating the shit out of!" Josh exclaimed.

"The name's Willam, and thats not the way its going to work," The man replied as the two men circled each other. Spencer just writhed on the ground, clutching at his face. Josh took a sudden step forward, the man recoiled slightly, Josh took this opportunity to lunge forward, looking to tackle the man. But Willam was a skilled fighter. He sidestepped, grabbing Josh about the waist and slamming him to the ground, knocking out his breath. Josh rolled to avoid the kick, scrambling back to his feet, slinking back to the edge of the ring.

Josh was waiting, examining his prey, trying to calculate the best option. Suddenly Willam came upon him, Josh barely had time to dive to the ground and roll from the lunge. Willam was launched into the crowd, who immediately threw him back into the ring. Willam ran at Josh again, this time catching his shirt with his left hand, punching with his right before pulling Josh to the ground. Willam grabbed Josh's arm, and lowered his face to it. Josh was horror-stricken as the man took a large bite out of his flesh, savoring the taste of the blood, Josh reached up and kicked the man in the face, sending him sliding across the floor, leaving a trail of Josh's blood. Josh clutched at his arm, the blood seeping through his fingers. He slowly stood up, now he was angry.

"What the hell is wrong with you?" Josh asked, "You nearly beat my friend to death, then you take a god damned bite out of my arm?" The maniac just looked at Josh, seething, blood bubbling from his mouth. Josh ran at him, unleashing pure rage. He jumped, landing on Willam, taking him forcefully to the ground. He punched the man across the face, a massive bruise forming instantly on his cheek, blood running from his nose. He rolled Josh off of him and kicked him in the face, breaking his nose and blackening his eye. Suddenly there was a commotion as somebody pushed through the crowd.

Willam was grabbed from behind, arms restrained. Alex held the psychopath firmly, pulling a knife out of his pocket. He tossed the knife to Josh, who flicked it open and moved forward on Willam. Suddenly there was shouting, and a gunshot rang out. A group of ten guards burst through the crowd, aiming rifles at the three men.

"Everybody down on the ground now! Hands behind your head, we will shoot!" One of the guards yelled. Josh dropped to his knees, hands behind his head. The knife clattered to the ground. Alex released Willam and got to his knees. Spencer managed to sit up on his knees. Suddenly Willam launched forward, kicking Josh in the face, sending him sprawling to the ground. Two guards rushed forward and restrained him.

Josh got to his feet and ran at Willam, punching him in the stomach while he was held. Two guards came forward and restrained Josh. The two men struggled against their captors, attempting to run at each other. Two guards grabbed Spencer and Alex, just in case.

"What the hell is going on here?" The General yelled, breaking into the ring. His eyes bulged at the blood spread on the floor and walls.

"It's Willam, Sir," Alex explained, "He went completely ape-shit! He took a chunk out of Josh's arm!"

"Well, who started the fight?" The General asked.

"Willam attacked Spencer," Josh replied.

"Actually, thats not true," Spencer coughed from the floor. Josh and Alex stared at him, amazed.

"What?" Josh asked.

"This bastard was bad mouthing you, Josh, said that you had no right to take control of the battle today, so I punched him in the face," Spencer replied.

"I don't care who started it. Half rations for the four of you, one month. This block is under detention for two months. You may only leave for meals and training sessions. I hope there will be no more fights. Guards, take Willam to solitary, one week sentence." And with that The General left the building. The guards dragged a screaming Willam away, Josh and Spencer were taken to the hospital, Alex went to bed.

Over the next two months, nothing spectacular occurred. Once a week there was a massive, block versus block battle, every day there was a block inspection, other than that there were classes and tests, once every three days a doctor would come and check Josh's arm. Josh, Alex and Spencer bonded while they were stuck in their block. Willam came back from solitary a different man. He was extremely polite, and even apologized for Josh's arm. In fact, he became so sincere, he was accepted into Josh's closer friend group. Every day Josh had an extensive conversation with Alexis out his window. She had become one of his best friends. He had given her his gun and ammunition to her, the searches had become more intense since the lockdown.

An illegal poker tournament began. A group of twenty men snuck out of their beds at night and crept into the bathrooms. Somebody had brought cards into the camp, that man was a genius. They played with straight up cash on the table, chips would be too complicated. Josh did extremely well in these games, partially because he was counting cards the whole time. They bet small, but every night Josh walked out with about three hundred dollars more.

THE PASSING GRADE

Josh never thought that he would survive the half rations, the training was so physically exhausting that by the time he was put on full rations he was nearly a skeleton. But finally, the two months of lockdown were over, and Josh stepped out into the sun as a free man again. He had found out that during their lockdown Block A had been locked down, and that the first set of grades had been announced. The instant he stepped out the doors Alexis ran up and hugged him.

"Where are the marks?" Josh asked. Alexis took his hand and led him to a wall with a large poster on it. His friends had followed him. Josh found Alex's name first.

"Yo, Alex, you're managing to keep an eighty six," Josh called. Alex double fist pumped the air, falling to his knees. Josh found Spencer, "Spencer, ninety four, try-hard." Spencer shrugged it off. "Um, Willam, you got a ninety two, and I have a.... ninety three! Yes!" Josh hugged Spencer, he thought he was going to fail.

"Who's first?" Alex asked.

"Some guy named... Demetri Eastguard. Hm, a D Block guy, he's got a 99.9," Josh replied.

"Thats not possible," Alex exclaimed.

"The next guy to him has a ninety seven, he's ruining the curve!" Josh commented, half laughing to himself. The group walked off, Willam stayed behind to read the rest of the list. He had told Josh he had some friends in B Block. He rejoined the group halfway through a spirited game of basketball. Josh and Alex swept the floor, twenty five to seven. They high fived, just being glad to be able to relax in the sun.

It was lunch. Josh filed through the line, waiting for a slab of meat and a bowl of soup, dreaming of a glass of lemonade. He took a seat at a table between Willam and Spencer. Alexis was sitting across from them with one of her friends. Mizuki slid in next to her, and Alex beside her. Josh suspected that he had been waiting in the crowd to sit next to her. Josh took a long swig of lemonade, trying to make an excuse for the inevitable flushing of his cheeks that occurred when he saw Alex making headway.

"So, how was lockdown?" Alexis asked, although she already knew from the conversations at the window.

"Actually not bad, just kinda missed running around outside of the training, we had a good underground game of p-" Josh hit Alex to make him shut up, a guard had just walked past the table. Josh needed to protect the large wad of cash in his pocket. After lunch they went back to playing basketball. Josh retired to his Block, Alex followed close behind him.

"Hey," Alex said suddenly, tapping Josh on the shoulder.

"Yeah?" Josh asked.

"I bought these from a guard earlier today, wanna celebrate the lift of the lockdown?" Alex asked, holding up two beers.

"We just got out, do you want to be locked back in?" Josh asked. Alex just looked at him, holding up the beers. "Fine," Josh admitted after a while. Alex threw him a beer, Josh popped the cap off on the wall as Ace had taught him. Alex was impressed. They slowly sipped the liquid, enjoying the taste. They talked about the camp, what they had done before they had been taken here, and what they planned to do after.

Suddenly the peaceful moment was broken by a blood-curdling scream from the building next to them. Josh dropped his beer, grabbed the revolver from under his pillow and slipped it into his belt, hidden under his shirt. He bolted out the door, followed closely by Alex. They burst into the Block D building. Everything seemed normal, but there was nobody in the room. Josh signaled for Alex to take the left side of bunks, and Josh took the right, pulling his revolver. All was silent. Josh slowly moved about the bunks, checking each one for a person. He could have sworn he saw a shadowy figure, but there was, alas, nobody there.

"Holy... Shit," Josh heard Alex exclaim from the end of the row. Josh ran the rest of the way, nearly slipping in a pool of blood. Alex was standing over a dead body, a single bullet hole to the head, the pistol in his hand, the same model the guards carried. There was a large puddle of blood around the head, and it was all over the clothing. The look on the man's face was one of peace, not fit to the scream that had broken the silence.

"Go get the guards, I'll stay here and see if the killer comes back," Josh ordered. Alex ran off. Josh dropped to his knees, ready to investigate. The face was the thing that stood out. The rest looked straight up suicide. Josh pulled gloves out of his pocket and slipped them onto his hands, so as not to leave fingerprints. He tilted the head to the left, then the right. Something caught the light. Josh looked closer, and saw a black, synthetic thread of material on the eyelid. Somebody had changed the facial expression. Josh pulled back the man's jacket, and took the wallet out of his breast pocket. He flipped it open, the I.D. read...

"No way," Josh breathed. It was Demetri Eastguard, top of the class. Josh replaced the wallet and folded the jacket back over. He continued to investigate until he heard the guards, escorted by Alex, charge through the front door of the building. Josh stood up, quickly removing the gloves from his hands. He had found no leads as to who was responsible. Whoever killed this poor bastard was careful.

"Well, look what the fish brought in," One of the guards exclaimed through a heavy mustache. Josh and Alex stood there for a second in confusion at what the man had just said, then snapped out of it and explained the situation.

"We heard a scream, so we came in here to investigate, found him dead," Josh explained.

"Why were you here when we got here?" The mustached guard asked.

"Making sure that the killer didn't come back, sir," Josh replied.

"Well, we get enough suicides here, wrap him up and toss him. Must have stolen a pistol from a guard, poor bastard. Who wants coffee?" The mustached guard asked.

"But... this is a murder!" Josh exclaimed.

"Murder? You talk murder around here, there's gonna be serious consequences," The guard warned Josh, darkness coming into his eyes.

"But... the scream!" Josh argued. The guard just glared him down before spinning on his heel and leaving the building. The other guards began to hoist the body, taking it out of the building. Josh and Alex left, shocked by the events. Josh was determined to track down the killer, but he would have to be quiet about it, he must avoid solitary at all costs.

CHAPTER FOUR

"Did you hear about it?" Josh asked Alexis, they were at the firing range with Alex.

"Yeah, that poor guy committed suicide. And after he came in top of the class, too!" Alexis replied as she peered down the telescope at the dummy some two miles away. Alex lay on the ground next to her, carefully adjusting his rifle. Josh leaned against the wall behind them, eating an apple.

"What if I told you it wasn't a suicide," Josh replied, taking another bite out of his apple.

"What? The official report said-"

"Screw the official report!" Josh exclaimed, throwing his apple on the ground. "The guards here are shitheads, pig-dogs that would rather let a murderer walk free than do any more work than they have to! They would rather let students who know the truth go insane than do a little detective work! The guards here are enough to drive one to murder, not that they would try to stop you! I mean," Josh started ranting. Alex tuned both of them out. He took a deep breath and squeezed the trigger. The loud gunshot silenced Josh. Alexis exclaimed seconds later.

"Headshot! How the hell do you do that?" She asked Alex, amazed.

"Long, hard nights at the range. I was in a specialized prison from age fourteen to sixteen. The only activity I enjoyed was sniping targets. Don't ask me why they let me have a rifle, but it damn near saved my life," Alex replied, pulling back the pin on the rifle. Josh pondered why they would have let him have a rifle in prison. Perhaps the I.E.M.F. had noticed him before... and tested him secretly...

"New target, one and a half clicks out, quarter click left of the last one," Alexis called. Alex looked down the scope. Josh walked up and peered down the telescope. She had chosen a hard target. It was a dummy on a fake motorcycle that moved back and forward at a realistic speed, it wore a helmet and bulletproof armor. Alex would have to hit it dead in the neck. Alex tweaked a dial on the scope, held his breath, and squeezed the trigger. Josh watched fake blood explode out of the dummy's neck half a second later.

"Amazing," Josh congratulated.

"Thats enough for one day, it's getting dark," Alex said, standing up. He began to disassemble the rifle. The parts fit nicely into the slots of the alligator case. Alex snapped it shut, sliding it back into it's place on the large wall of weapons. The three walked the long path back to camp, the bell for dinner was just sounding. The three of them were joined by Mizuki and Spencer. They ate well, devouring a large steak and a serving of mashed potatoes and steamed vegetables. *We deserve good food,* Josh thought to himself, *After all the other hell we go through.*

"So, tell us about this murder," Spencer asked. Josh put a finger to his lips, telling Spencer to keep quiet about it. A guard walked by the table, rifle in hand. He seemed to have not heard it. That was one good thing about the volume in the cafeteria. Willam suddenly sat at the table.

"What are we talking about?" He asked before taking a long swig of Earl Grey.

"The suicide," Mizuki replied.

"The murder, actually," Josh corrected, "The one in Block D."

"That was officially called a suicide!" Willam exclaimed, Josh looked around for guards, before going on.

"I found hard evidence that it was a murder," Josh explained. The group leaned in, food forgotten, intrigued by the mystery.

"Well, go on," Alex prompted.

"First of all, you guys need to keep this all quiet. Conspiracy and distrusting guards earns you a whole month in solitary, so my ass is on the line," Josh asked, shoving his thumb against his chest. The group nodded. "Okay. The first thing wrong with the suicide theory is the scream. There was a horrifying, terrible scream that erupted into the air, which is what brought Alex and I into the Block. Somebody who kills themselves would not scream, there's a risk you'd be found before you died. Also, the look of peace on his face with which the guards are basing their entire argument, it wasn't natural. There were traces of foreign fibers on the eyelids, from what I can gather it is the same material as our battle gloves. The victim shot himself with a guards pistol, he could have easily bought one for self defense. But, if somebody shot him with the same model of pistol, at the time the victim drew it, it would look like he shot himself. Another thing, Alex, if you would please put a hand to your head, as if you were going to shoot yourself," Josh asked. Alex raised his fingers to his temple.

"See, his hand is on the side of his head. The same side as his dominant hand. Now Alex, please try to shoot yourself in the other side of the head, using the same arm." Alex struggled for a bit before admitting defeat. "Our victim was shot in the left side of the head, but his file, which I pulled last night, stated quite clearly that he was right handed. I returned to the scene of the crime after the body was removed, but before they cleaned the blood. There was a strange circular pattern where the body had fallen, as if residual force from spinning to see someone enter the room caused the body to spiral to the floor. There was a blood splotch on a bunk a few feet behind him, meaning that the angle of bullet entry would line up perfectly with the door. But that's all I got," Josh finally finished. The group leaned back, impressed by Josh's deduction.

"Do you have any leads?" Willam asked, taking a long pull of his tea.

"No, the evidence doesn't point anywhere, there are two guys in A Block that I don't think are too stable, but I don't want to go to them, they seem a bit too buddy-buddy with the guards," Josh replied.

"I think I may have a plan... Josh, how much money did you end up walking out of poker with last night?" Alex asked.

"About seven thousand," Josh replied, slightly boasting to Mizuki.

"That should be enough. You see the old guard standing by the door, smoking?" Alex asked.

"Yeah," Josh replied.

"He's told me that for ten thousand dollars he'll put a guy in solitary for a month. You give him twenty five thousand, he'll see those two guys get put in. We could all cash in," Alex informed Josh. Josh was troubled by this, he knew of the horrors that solitary held, Willam had not told him, but his drastic personality change and silence about the topic told Josh enough.

"No," Josh decided, "I can't send them there without definite proof, I wouldn't condemn an innocent man to that torture."

"You can pay that guard off to keep an eye on them at least," Willam retorted.

"Yeah, thats probably a good idea," Josh replied, standing up. He leaned in to Alexis, whispering "I've left my gun under my coat on the bench. Wait thirty seconds after I leave, then slip it into your pocket and follow me and the guard, if anything looks shifty, safety off." Josh did an over dramatic bow to the table, mostly directed at Mizuki. He made his way across the busy room, weaving between the tables and various groups. Out of the corner of his eye he saw Alexis stand up, his coat over her arm.

"Hello, sir," Josh announced, saluting the guard. The guard stared at him through weathered eyes. He blew smoke in Josh's face.

"What?" The old guard asked. Josh leaned forward and whispered in the guard's ear, and the guard turned and left the building. Josh followed him out, Alexis a good distance behind. The guard came to a stop at the corner of a building, cigar still in his mouth.

"How can I help you?" He asked.

"There's two guys in Block A, I don't know their names, but they look pretty shifty and wear yellow bandanas around their arms during free time," Josh reported.

"Yeah, I know the guys," The guard replied.

"For the right price, will you keep an eye on 'em for me? Restrict their movements, make sure that there's always a guard in their vicinity. How much will that be?" Josh asked.

"Five thousand, 'cause I'm putting my ass on the line here," The guard said.

"Four thousand, and you get me ten rounds of revolver ammunition," Josh countered.

"Four thousand five hundred, and its five rounds," The guard came back.

"Four thousand three hundred, and its seven rounds!" Josh returned.

"Fine, its a deal," The guard agreed. Josh handed over two thousand one hundred fifty dollars.

"You'll get the other half when the rounds are in my hands," Josh informed the guard, this brought an unhappy look to his face, but he accepted it and left. Josh turned the corner to the barrel of a gun in his face. By instinct he grabbed the barrel of the gun and twisted it, the handle of the weapon slipping out of it's wielder's hand, Josh flipped it around, grabbing onto the handle, pointing the gun in the face of Josh's attacker.

"Jesus!" Alexis exclaimed, "Take a joke Josh!" Josh looked down and realized he was holding his own gun, and the brunette hair in front of him belonged to his friend. Her face was partially covered by shadow.

"Don't do that again. *I don't want to get shot with my own gun,*" Josh said, holstering the weapon and taking his jacket from Alexis, slipping it on.

"Is it just me, or is it actually getting kind of cold out here?" Alexis asked. Josh hadn't noticed it, but he was kind of chilly.

"It's a nice break from the torturing sun," Josh commented. If only they knew of the cold winter to come. They returned to the dining hall to see that their friends had left. Alexis and Josh made their way back to the yard, they realized that it was time to retire to their respective Blocks, they gave their goodbyes and departed. Josh, Alex and Spencer entered the bathrooms, there was a poker game going on. Josh and Alex sat at the table, Spencer left to read. There was an author in the Block, he was constantly writing in his journal, and gave the stories to Spencer. It was a good system. Josh was dealt, they were playing five stud two draw poker.

Josh quickly glanced at his hand. A three, four, five, seven, king, two spades two hearts one diamond. Josh felt a tapping at his foot. He and Alex had worked out a secret code. After about twenty seconds of quick taps, Josh found out that Alex held three spades and two hearts, the numbers didn't matter, he didn't have a six. Josh quickly tapped back to wait until the first change to start cheating. Josh matched the fifty dollar bet and raised to one hundred. Alex matched. The bet came around again, this time Josh matched, Alex matched, and the cards changed. Josh put out his king of hearts, and received a five of clubs.

He felt Alex place two cards on his leg. Josh quickly flipped two spades into his sleeve before slipping the other two cards into his hand. He now had shit, but he knew that Alex had a flush. He snapped the two spades out of his sleeve and placed them on Alex's leg, who slipped them into his hand. Nobody had noticed. Now Alex would lay low, matching or raising by one, and Josh would go all out, the two would split the money later. Josh was secretly keeping track of the cards. There was a good chance that... no, that would be too lucky.

Alex matched the twenty dollar bet. Josh came into his role and raised to one hundred. The person to his left folded. The next few matched, it came back around to Josh without being raised, so there was another card change. Josh hoped, he put out three cards, and got back three. Before he lifted them, he did a quick count of the odds. He held a four and a five of hearts. The odds of it were... nearly impossible, but better than they could have been. The official odds... one in two hundred thirty five. He lifted the cards. He had beat the odds. six, seven, eight of hearts. Josh had a straight flush, good to beat or back up Alex.

Josh decided not to tell Alex of this development, seeing as Alex may take it as a move to start raising. Alex matched the hundred fifty dollar bet, Josh raised to two hundred. The pile of bills in the center of the table was ominous, the shadow cast far across the room. He did a quick tally. He had counted a total of forty six bets, and if his memory served him correctly, there was ten thousand, two hundred fifty dollars in the pot. The bet came around again, Alex matched. Josh went for it.

"All in," Josh called, shoving his bills into the center of the table. Fold, fold, fold, fold, fold, fold, fold, fold, then a man matched. Josh had noticed him around the Block, he kept to himself, a shadowy character. He pushed his bills into the center. Fold, fold, fold, fold, Alex matched, shoving his bills in.

"Gentlemen, show your cards," The dealer called, excited by the events. Alex slapped down his flush, beaming. The man across the table smirked, and laid down a straight flush. Alex stood up, kicking his chair across the room. He believed that he and Josh were broke. Josh quickly checked the man's cards. It was a straight flush, of clubs, two three four five six. Josh smirked as he lay down his cards. His strait was higher than the man's. Alex ran up and hugged Josh, amazed by the play. The man across the table just stared at Josh's cards, dumbstruck. The other men in the room were going ape shit. They yelled, screamed, amazed at the game. Josh scooped up the cash and organized it all, fifteen thousand nine hundred and forty dollars.

    He split it up and gave half to Alex, the room was beginning to calm down. Josh quickly went and hid the cash in his bunk, taking only two thousand dollars to play the next round. He would soon be very glad he did this. The next round began, Josh didn't care about his cards, as a gentleman he had to stay in one more round for decencies sake. Bets, Josh put in twenty bucks, Alex put in twenty, it was a rather boring game in comparison. Suddenly there was a crash out in the Block, followed by screams and shouts.

    Josh knew what was coming. He threw his cards across the table and shoved the bills in his pocket. A group of twenty guards burst through the doors, wielding batons. They beat down the players nearest them, filing into the room and belting the gamblers about the head. A guard came up to Josh and brought his baton down on his collarbone, Josh didn't fight back, it would only make it worse. The blow hurt like hell, throbbing and burning as he crumpled to the ground. The guard kicked him in the stomach.

    Josh curled up, the pain was too much. He clutched at his head, feeling blood. The guard grabbed him by the collar and hoisted him to his feet, then slammed him back down on the ground in a sitting position. Somebody had knocked over the table, the bills were blowing about the room. A commanding voice yelled above the commotion, and the guards and troops fell silent.

"What the hell is going on here?" The General asked, standing in the doorway.

"Illegal poker game, sir!" A guard replied, dropping a troop on the ground, who grunted with the impact.

"Interesting. You think this block would be on good behavior after their lockdown. Now tell me, who is responsible for this game?" The General asked.

"I am," A man reported, stepping forward.

"No, I am," Another said.

"Screw those guys, I started this," A third man came forward.

"No, I," The shadowy man who had just lost all his money came forward.

"No, I," Josh called,

"Stop this before it goes any further. This entire situation is far too cliche. The Spartacus move is overdone anyway. I think it will be enough punishment if we take your cards and money, and leave you with your wounds. Guards, you may beat them for two more minutes, then please meet for a drink in the dining hall. Au revoir," The General said, turning and leaving as the beating continued. Josh clenched his jaw and tensed his muscles, counting down the seconds.

Whack, whack, whack. The bruises formed near instantly, blood dripped from a broken nose. Josh got to one hundred and two seconds before a kick landed on his jaw, effectively cracking it. Josh felt the blood stream into his mouth, the warm, coppery taste flowing over his tongue, past his teeth and down his chin. The guard hit him again over the head and he lost consciousness.

*   *   *

"Jesus this looks bad," A voice called from somewhere far away in the darkness. Josh recognized the voice, and slowly started to come to. It was the voice of Mizuki. Josh slowly opened his eyes, tentatively letting in the light. He saw two dark figures standing over him, he could not feel his face.

"Alexis? Mizuki?" Josh asked. The two figures nodded, slowly coming into focus. He was back in the hospital, a bandage about his jaw, and patches over his body. The time, said the clock, was one AM. "What are you two doing here?" He asked, astounded by the time.

"It's eight AM, Josh, that clock is broken," Mizuki replied.

"Eight? Oh shit, I have a psychology lesson now!" Alexis exclaimed, grabbing a bag from the floor and dashing out the door. Josh looked around. It was just he and Mizuki left. There was tension in the air.

"The guards were pretty rough on you guys. Alex has a bad leg now, he's on crutches," Mizuki informed Josh.

"Speaking of Alex..." Josh started. He wondered what kind of meds the doctors had him on to be thinking of doing this. "I really, really like you Mizuki. And so does Alex. We have sort of had an unspoken tournament for you in the past months, but if he finds out I told you any of this, he's literally going to kill me. We need to keep this a secret for right now," Mizuki was taken aback, processing the information.

Josh sat there awkwardly, knowing he had made a tactical error. Suddenly, without warning, Mizuki reached forward, placing a hand on the side of Josh's face. She brought her head down, and they kissed. It was very passionate, their lips interlocked, her skin was soft and smooth. Josh closed his eyes, taking in the experience. The pains of his body melted away. The kiss lasted a few seconds before Mizuki pulled back, cheeks flushed.

"I... really need to go," She said hurriedly, running out of the room, leaving Josh satisfied yet guilty. He felt as if he had cheated in his competition with Alex. He slowly stood up from the bed, testing his weight on his legs. He was still dressed in his casual dress, and blood stained the neck area of the shirt. Josh made his way out of the room, he passed a mirror, seeing his reflection for the first time in months. A light layer of hair had begun to grow back atop his scalp, heavy dark bags hung under his eyes. His nose was deformed from several breakings, his left eye blackened. His face had become much slimmer and more muscular. A light stubble lined his chin and jawline.

Josh exited the building, a definite chill was in the air. He decided that he would buy a warmer jacket from a guard before the weather got any colder. He made his way across the yard to where Spencer and Willam were playing basketball, Alex stood on the sidelines, watching the game intently, leaning on a cane. A heavier soldier Josh did not recognize stood next to Alex, enjoying the game. Josh came up beside him, his breath clinging to the cold air.

"Good game, William's up by one point. Spencer's gotten a lot better since the start of camp. He's gotten four three pointers, dunked twice, and gotten a few decent trick shots," Alex informed Josh.

"Standard," Josh replied as Willam dunked on Spencer, the ball shooting through the hoop and hitting him on the head.

"Ouch!" Spencer called, rubbing his head.

"Well, I think that just about makes it a game," Willam bragged, walking off the court triumphantly. Josh rubbed his jaw, feeling slowly returning, it hurt like hell. The man watching the game took up the ball and began shooting hoops, alone.

A short distance away in A Block, a lonely man sat at a desk, writing a letter home. He would pay off a guard to send it, it would be costly but worth it. He reported the state of the camp, what his life was like, what classes were like, but most importantly that he had placed second out of all the students. Suddenly there was a smash as the doors to the Block banged open.

"Hello, Chris," The voice at the door said menacingly. The man at the desk shoved the paper into his pocket, coming to his feet. The chair clattered to the floor. The shadow of the man in the door was wielding a pistol.

"How do you know my name?" Chris asked the shadowy man. The door shut, the figure moved toward Chris. Chris backed into the building, yelling for someone. The building was empty. The murderer had perfect timing once again. He came up to Chris and pulled a length of rope from the desk. He pocketed the gun and began to tie a noose around one of the posts that ran along the ceiling of the Block.

"Put your head in the rope unless you want a bullet to the brain. This way, you may be found before you die," The man demanded, pulling a chair up under the rope. Chris got up on the chair and pulled the rope down around his head. A tear streamed down his cheek. The man walked up, examining his prey. His adrenaline was pumping... the power... the thrill... the control... *look at me now Dad.*

"I really do enjoy this," The man informed the weakling standing on the chair, "It is just such fun," The man added as he kicked out the chair. The body dropped, his feet stopping an inch above the ground. The poor bastard's neck hadn't broken. He struggled as he hung there, slowly suffocating to death. The killer left the building, smirking at the prospect of his next kill.

CHAPTER FIVE

Josh felt the sweat drip down his brow, the wire cutters in his hand becoming slippery with the tension. He looked down. Among the mess of cables, resistors, circuit boards and scraps of metal, he had narrowed it down to two wires, one red, one green. One lead from the power source to a bit on unidentified metal, and another lead from the power source to a different unknown piece. Josh glanced at the timer, fifteen seconds remaining. If the timer hit zero, or if Josh set it off incorrectly, a neurotoxin would be released into the room filled with students. Those with weaker hearts could die, the others would be revived but near death.

"Please, make yourself comfortable while I warm up the neurotoxin emitters," The voice of the teacher came over a loudspeaker from somewhere, as if the situation wasn't stressful enough. Josh made a decision. He quickly reached down and sniped the red wire. There was a second of pause before a light turned green and the door slid open. The group collectively let out their breath.

"Class dismissed," The voice called. The students filed out of the room, wiping the moist from their brow and laughing nervously at the experience. Three steps from the door Josh was caught by the arm. He turned to see Alex, out of breath, red in the cheeks, his cane hanging limply in his hand, unused. Josh made a mental note of this fact.

"There's been another murder," Alex informed Josh. Josh went white, breaking into a cold sweat. Alex ran off, sprinting across the yard, cane forgotten. Josh followed close behind. It was so cold, he could barely move his hands. Frost on the grass... there was a thin line of ice around the pond. Josh saw the yellow tape across the door of Block A from the edge of the basketball court. Soon he was ducking under the tape, Alex close behind.

Josh stared up into the glassy, dead eyes of the body hanging, slowly rotating. The face was blue, skin bunched up around the neck. The cause of death was suffocation, not a broken neck. The chair was knocked half way across the room. It had been kicked by someone else, not by the man hanging there. There was a half finished note on the desk near him. Josh glanced over it. The man had stopped writing halfway through a word, and it wasn't a suicide note, it was a letter home. It brought tears to Josh's eyes.

Josh stepped closer to the body, scrutinizing the features. Small growth on the upper right middle finger. The man was right handed, and wrote a lot. This information was useless to Josh. After several minutes of examination, Josh was certain the man was murdered. Again, no clues as to the murderer.

"Jesus christ!" A voice called from behind Josh. He turned to see Willam standing behind him, eyes locked with the hanging body, "Another in the chain," Willam added.

"What?" Josh asked.

"This guy, I am in a psychology class with him, er, was. His name is Chris, and he was second best grade in the camp," Willam explained. Josh got a sinking feeling in his stomach, he knew what was happening, what was going to happen, and how it was going to end.

"We have a serial killer," Josh exclaimed. The room fell silent, all eyes locked on Josh. There was a collective gasp at the news. Willam placed a hand on Josh's shoulder and turned him around. The General was standing directly behind Josh, face red, seething.

Josh soon found himself in The General's office, sitting across the desk from the bulky man, staring each other down. It was a very nice office, elegantly decorated with lavish red silk and marble. It seemed like a room the Pope would officiate from. Josh could only imagine The Master's office.

"Stone, I'm getting quite tired of your insubordination. It seems to me that you will do anything you can in this camp to get yourself beaten, screamed at, punished, or have your rations cut. It almost makes me think that you *want* to go to solitary. Thinking you can escape from there, maybe? Well let me tell you something. Escape from here is *impossible!*" The General yelled, spit flying onto Josh's face. "This facility is surrounded by a fence carrying enough volts to fry your family tree all the way back to your grandfather. Our guards are top notch, taken from the Marines. You *can't* get out, Josh. Now, allow me to repeat myself, and this is the last time I do so before your ass is hauled off to *solitary*. These are suicides, Josh. Not murders. Some people just can't take the heat, they take the easy way out. If there was a murderer here, the guards would have taken him away already. I'm tired of your insubordination Josh, just stop."

"No, I'm tired of you not giving a *shit* about *your troops,*" Josh yelled back, standing up, his chair flying across the room.

"Josh!" The General yelled.

"No, god dammit, you let me talk!" Josh yelled, "I hate to ruin your perfect little world, but there is a psychopathic *murderer* in this camp! And you and your *special* guards, aren't doing shit about it! And if you aren't, I will. I will catch this guy, before he kills again. I hate you, *sir,* you pretend to be a father figure, but really you're a dictator, just enjoying our pain, watching us suffer gets you off, doesn't it! You are a horrible leader!" Josh yelled.

"Josh, this is unacceptable!" The General yelled back.

"No, you are unacceptable! I can barely stand to look at you, you lying shit!" Josh yelled.

"You're just acting out against authority figures because your father died in that car crash!" The General screamed at Josh.

"At least I know who my father is!" Josh shrieked back. The General slapped Josh across the face, hard. Josh spun on his heel and fell to the floor, his cheek catching a wall mounted sword on his way down. He crumpled to the floor, blood streaming down his neck and onto his shirt. He was amazed that he had lashed out like that, after his years of military based training. He knew that the remark was uncalled for, but in that man... he saw everything wrong with the world. Josh got to his feet, staring down The General.

"Fuck you. People are being killed. I hope you like their blood on your hands, as well as mine," Josh announced, turning and throwing open the door. Josh stormed through and slammed the door behind him. Alex was sitting beside the door, he must have been listening to the entire exchange.

"That was incredible, Josh!" Alex exclaimed, handing Josh a facecloth. Josh wiped the blood from his chin and neck.

"Thanks," Josh replied, feeling at the cut. It was deep, it would definitely scar.

"Why did that father remark of yours bring such a rise?" Alex asked.

"His mother was raped, he was the result," Josh explained, "I figured it out within ten seconds of being in that office."

"What gave it away?" Alex asked.

"Little things," Josh replied. They exited into the yard, the cold reminding Josh again to get himself a coat. He and Alex parted ways, Alex going to an accuracy test, Josh heading left to find his guard. He spotted the Block A brothers from far away, and knew that the guard would be hidden somewhere near. After thirty seconds of searching, Josh found his man leaning against a tree, behind a bush.

"I need something else," Josh broke the ice, the old man taking a puff of his cigar.

"Hm?" The old man asked.

"I need a trench coat. A nice thin one, down about my knees, dark brown, with a collar. It'll fetch you five hundred bucks atop the price of the jacket," Josh demanded. The old man nodded. Three days later, Josh returned to his bunk from a brutal battle to find several revolver rounds wrapped in his large brown trench coat. Josh slipped it on; it was heavy on his shoulders, but also quite warm. For some reason, it made Josh feel like he could take on the world. Several yards away, Alex sat in the cafeteria with Alexis, talking over coffee.

"Did you hear about Spencer and Mizuki?" Alex asked.

"No..." Alexis began, taking a sip of her coffee.

"Well Josh and I saw him hitting on her, it was hilarious! He was doing such a horrible job, as if he could get her anyway!" Alex snorted, taking a large swig of his coffee. Alexis burst out laughing.

"Really?" She asked.

"Yeah! I mean, could you imagine those two together?" Alex replied. The two laughed for a while.

"You know, I'm amazed that you would make that joke," Alexis replied, calming down.

"What? Why?" Alex asked.

"Well, because you're into Mizuki, right?" Alexis asked.

"What? How did you know?" Alex asked, anger building.

"Well, Mizuki told me... I shouldn't say anything else," Alexis replied, turning away. Suddenly Alex had pulled a knife, flipping it open and stabbing it into the table.

"Tell me how," Alex growled.

"Josh told Mizuki that you and he both liked her when he was in the hospital after the raid. Apparently they kissed," Alexis replied, scared by the blade.

"That son of a bitch!" Alex suddenly yelled, drawing looks from across the room. "He broke the rules of our agreement! I'm gonna kill him... I can't believe he would go behind my back like that!"

"Alex calm down... what have I done? I never should have told you that... Shit!" Alexis exclaimed, pulling at her hair, head lowered.

"I won't kill him... but I will make him regret it," Alex growled, pocketing his knife.

"I'll tell him you know, I don't want this to break your friendship," Alexis said, trying to mend her mistake.

"No, we're good enough friends that this won't tear us apart. I'll tell him, we won't talk for a couple days, and then we'll be fine," Alex retorted.

"Are you sure?" Alexis asked.

"Yes, I'm sure. If you were the one to tell him, God that would be a bloody mess," Alex replied, standing up, taking his coffee with him. "Thanks for letting me know, Alexis," Alex added as he left. Alexis questioned her morals as she chugged the rest of her coffee. Alex found Josh talking with Spencer in the yard.

"How much do you love hotdogs?" Spencer began. Even from a distance, Alex could see Josh settling in to deal with a very long period of drowning Spencer out. "I think that they are literally one of the best breakthroughs in food since, and I know this is cliché but its true, sliced bread. I mean the bun in a containment unit for the meat, as well as a good vessel for condiments and the like. Plus, the linear design is perfect for easy eating, and it's also like a progress bar. And unlike a burger, when you go to eat it it doesn't block your entire view, just the line down your nose!"

"I think you're eating burgers wrong," Josh interjected before Spencer went off again.

"That reminds me of sliced bread. It's so much simpler than having to slice it yourself for breakfast... it cuts down morning time by like nine percent. That might not sound like a lot, but in the world of statistics it is. Plus, it would have always crumbled and fallen apart under the knife, I'm assuming... anyway..."

"Josh!" Alex called, saving him. Josh waved to Alex and ran up the hill to him, away from the talking machine.

"What's up?" Josh asked.

"Nice coat, by the way," Alex complimented.

"Thanks," Josh replied.

"We need to talk, Josh, have you got a moment?" Alex began.

"Guys!" Willam yelled from far away, Josh and Alex turned, Willam was running up the hill to them, Spencer close on his heels.

"What? I really need to talk to Josh about something!"Alex raged.

"The new grades were just posted... and the guy highest on the list was just found dead," Willam reported. The world seemed to melt around Josh. His brain kicked into overdrive, visions of the first two bodies and the evidence he had seen, the faces of everybody he had met, everything that had happened, trying to make connections. So many connections, Josh fell to his knees, clutching at his head. He could hear his heart pounding, each beat sending a wave of pain through his overheating brain.

"God... Just STOP!" Josh yelled at himself, falling on his side. It began to snow. The lines in Josh's head drew more complex, tiny observations he had made before, becoming more prominent, drawing more lines... this man is connected to this one to that one to her to him to them... the picture of bubbling, blistering flesh glowed prominently in front of all the other business... but what did it mean? Alex had dropped to his knees, placing a hand on Josh's forehead.

"What's wrong?" Alex asked. Josh squeezed his eyes shut, blocking out anything but the worlds in his head.

"Oh, God! MAKE IT STOP!" Josh yelled, pressing his temples to the point of bruising. The people filed by in his mind, backed by black splotched with red and yellows. The two dead bodies... the letter, the circles in the blood... the revolver... suddenly Josh's eyes flew open, the pain had fallen away.

"Take me to the body," Josh demanded, getting to his feet. Willam lead the three men away... toward the battle grounds. They came to the entrance of the field, the large gates locked. A stretcher was set up, a black sheet over it. Guards milled around the area, several troops where in the crowd as well. Josh and Alex came up to the stretcher and threw back the sheet. They were met with a nasty sight. A pulp of skin, blood, organs and bone was heaped on the stretcher, barely recognizable as human. Alex held back from vomiting, turning away from the remains. He decided he would have his talk with Josh at a later date.

"No! This is no good! I can't get any evidence off this!" Josh screamed, kicking a nearby rock. He tapped a guard on the shoulder. "What happened here?" Josh asked.

"We found this poor guy at the bottom of a cliff. Mangled like this when we got to him. Must have tripped, poor bastard. Just made the top of his class, too," The guard replied, disinterested with the business. Josh was furious at himself for not having solved the mystery earlier.

"So... you would catch the man before he struck again?" A familiar voice called from behind Josh. Josh clenched his fists, a vein pulsing on his forehead. He turned.

"General," Josh growled. "You may be Ace's brother, and you may be doing what you can for me, but I don't respect you. I don't love you the way I love Ace, and I sure as hell don't look up to you like I do him. I recommend you leave this place before I punch you in the face."

"I recommend that you holster your fists before you get thrown in solitary," The General growled back.

"If you put him in solitary, we'll kill you and every guard in the immediate premises," Spencer growled, a little too loudly. All the guards drew their guns. Alex, Willam and Spencer stepped forward to defend Josh.

"Are you threatening a revolt?" The General asked, the guards cocked their rifles.

"Technically, you are," Alex spat back. The other students in the area had fled, not wanting to be held accountable for the incident.

"Also, didn't you just admit that this was a murder?" Willam asked, quoting the general: "You would catch this man before he struck again?"

"No... This poor son of a bitch fell from the cliff," The General snapped back.

"He was pushed. We have a serial killer on our hands, sir!" Josh yelled. The General stared at Josh.

"Nice scar you have there, Stone," The General snapped, Josh felt the thick line of developing scar tissue that ran along his jaw.

"We're done here," Josh stated coldly. He walked away, followed closely by Alex, Spencer and Willam.

"Jesus that was intense," Spencer sighed.

"He won't put me in solitary, he can't. His brother would have him demoted. He would need a really good reason to put me in to stay out of trouble with Ace," Josh informed his friends. None of them knew who Ace was, but they didn't dare to ask. Back in the block, the four men sat on Josh's bed, saddened by the day's events.

"We need to take action against this psychopath," Josh broke the silence. The other men nodded. "Alex, tomorrow I want you to interrogate the top ten students on the list, see if there is anything shifty going on there. Spencer, I'll need you to distract the guards around Alex so that he can work in peace. Willam, I need you to follow the top remaining student all day, every day, for the next month. If anybody shady comes up to him, let him at the guy, just make sure you get a good look at him. Got your roles?" Josh asked. The men nodded.

"And what will you be doing?" Alex asked.

"What I do best," Josh replied, "Observing."

CHAPTER SIX

The lone man sat at the park bench, reading a textbook intently. A cool breeze blew through the yard, rustling leaves and turning the pages of his book. He heard an unnatural crunch of a twig breaking and looked up quickly, afraid for his safety. The stranger's face was shadowed by the tree he stood beside. He moved forward, his face revealed. He swooped into the seat.

"Hello there. Congratulations on the ninety nine percent!" Alex said to the man sitting across the table from him. The man looked scared.

"You're going to kill me aren't you?" The man asked, frightened.

"What? No... A mind like yours is too precious to exterminate. But I'm here to find out who is killing people. Do you know?" Alex asked. The man shook his head. "Has anybody dangerous or insane looking approached you recently?"

"Um... not that I can remember, and I'm sure keeping a good eye out for it," The man replied, wringing his wrists. Alex noticed this.

"Listen, I'm on your side here, man. I just want to protect you and the other gifted troops in this place. Do you know anything?" Alex asked again.

"Well, there was a guy who has been at the scene of every crime, really intently looking at stuff, acting kind of strange," The guy replied.

"Yeah, that's Josh. He's a friend of mine," Alex informed the man. "Or at least... he used to be."

"What do you mean?" The man asked.

"Well... he went behind my back a few days ago... told the girl I like that he and I both liked her. See, we had this agreement that we would have a fair competition for her and that we would... you know what? Why am I telling you this?" Alex asked.

"It makes you more relatable and approachable. It's a good interrogation technique," The man replied.

"I wasn't asking you seriously," Alex corrected.

"And reliability lost. You really aren't too good at this, are you?" The man asked.

"I'm good enough to know that you are helping me with my interrogation skills because you believe that our intelligence levels are differential enough that I would not be able to use them on you. You're the killer, because you're helping me interrogate you. Anybody else wouldn't want me too dive to deep. You want me to establish your own cover. Nice plan, bad execution. I'm not as stupid as you think, am I?" Alex asked,

"Sometimes," The man replied, leaning across the table, bringing his face close to Alex's, "Over thinking something so much that it turns into a convoluted conspiracy theory can be mistaken for intelligence. But you seem like a nice enough guy, so I'll be frank with you. I am not the killer, nor do I know who it is."

"Exactly what the killer would say. He's a psychopath. He may not even know that he is the killer. And now that I've said that, I realize that interrogation would be pointless. So you are Schrodinger's POI, you are both the killer, and not the killer, at the same time," Alex theorized, slightly confusing himself.

"And with that, you have hit the nail on the head. The murderer is obviously psychopathic, common among the serial, and may not even know that he is the murderer. So your exploits in these little discussions are pointless. Have a nice day," The man concluded, beginning to stand up.

"Not so fast. Nice try, murderer-mc-insanity-pants," Alex chimed like a child. The man sat back down.

"Now that's just immature," The man scolded.

"It got you back here though, didn't it?" Alex replied.

"What do you want? I've told you literally everything I know!" The man exclaimed, "And I don't want to be here much longer, if the guards see this they'll think I'm in on the conspiracy."

"I need to go for a second, but if you're not here when I get back, you are a dead man," Alex warned. He got up and sprinted down to the battle field. He hoped the fence, landing in a roll. He jogged along the main path for about five minutes before he came to the lip of a large cliff. A rope was tied to a tree, which lead over the edge. Alex grabbed tightly onto the rope and repelled halfway down the cliff.

"Hello, Alex!" Josh called from far below.

"Hello!" Alex yelled back, repelling to the bottom.

"What's up?" Josh asked.

"My witness knows something he isn't telling me, and I can't get through to him!" Alex called. Josh began to climb back up the rope. Alex climbed back to the top.

"Find anything interesting?" Alex asked once Josh was all the way up.

"These footprints here prove that there was a scuffle on this ridge. It wasn't accidental; see these two large indents here? The man was held over the cliff for sometime before he was dropped. This also proves that our murderer really, *really* enjoys his kills," Josh reported, giddy at the news.

"It scares me how happy you are about this," Alex replied. The two set off into the bush. Minutes later, Josh and Alex came back to the park table, the man still sitting there. Josh pushed back the end of his trench coat as he sat.

"Hello there, sir. My name is Joshua Stone, and I'm going to jump into your head now," Josh introduced himself. Alex walked a few paces away. He could not hear what they were saying, and in respect for Josh he did not read their lips. Two minutes later the man burst into tears, yelling and throwing his arms around randomly before he collapsed on the table, weeping.

"I have what we need. Cancel the other interrogations," Josh reported.

"Josh... That man is going one hundred in psychology... what did you say to him?" Alex asked. Josh just smiled at Alex, then turned and walked away, leaving Alex confused and terrified. Later that night, Alex, Josh, Willam and Spencer snuck out of their Block, which was no easy job. They had one objective. Kill Alexis.

FOUR HOURS PRIOR

"Gentlemen, there comes a time in every man's life where he must make a decision, to benefit the greater good, but at dire expense to the individual. Tonight, we must make that decision, and act upon it," Josh began. He, Alex, Spencer, and Willam were gathered in the yard, sitting on the grass in a circle. They had made sure that nobody else was near.

"What do we need to do, Josh?" Alex asked, the others were stern faced, serious about the actions ahead, and unafraid to face them.

"Thanks to the brilliant interrogation skills of Alex, we had a lead on the murderer. Although it was hard to believe, we had to accept the fact. I then sent Willam out to investigate the person. The evidence he returned was as disturbing as it was rock solid and impenetrable. Alexis, our friend, is the murderer. This is an unavoidable fact. She is eleventh on the list of top students, and is obviously killing anybody with a higher grade than her, hoping to finish top of the class. Tonight, we will sneak out of our bunks, out of our Block, into hers, and murder her in her sleep. It is the path that must be taken," Josh briefed the men in a loud, steady voice. He saw the others cower, afraid of the certainty.

"Josh, this is murder your talking about. Forget the moral objections or the fact that the person you are talking about killing is one of our friends, one of your best friends, but also, we could land the rest of our stay here in solitary. Thats seven months, Josh. They say that nobody comes out of there after two months sane. There's no way we can pull this off," Willam objected.

"She's already murdered three people, maybe even four now, Willam. Think of how many people we will be saving by silencing her," Alex replied.

"How solid is your evidence? Couldn't we be killing an innocent person? To simply put someone in jail the proof must be beyond a reasonable doubt, but killing someone? Thats an entirely different level of certainty," Spencer argued.

"The evidence that Willam has brought forth does bring us beyond a reasonable doubt, along with the confession from Alex's *witness*. He *saw* Alexis push the man off that cliff," Josh retorted.

"Possibly lying witness aside for now, what is this evidence?" Spencer asked.

"You know that weird guy in Block A that bought a camera from a guard on the first day and hasn't stopped taking pictures yet?" Willam asked.

"Yeah," Spencer and Alex replied in unison.

"He got a picture of Alexis entering Block A with a length of rope in the timezone that Josh set for that murder. The date was saved with the photo. He snapped another picture of her leaving later, pale, the rope gone. These pictures are roughly ten minutes apart," Willam replied, handing the two photos to Spencer, who looked them over.

"I guess... you guys are right," Spencer whimpered, face pale white and ghostly. "This is pretty solid proof... and if she's a serial killer, she needs to be taken out. But how the hell do you plan to pull this off?" Spencer asked.

"The plan is simple, the execution extremely difficult," Josh began.

"Easier said than done," Alex repeated. Josh went through the plan. Ten minutes later the men stood up, shaking hands in secrecy, and set off to dinner. They met Alexis and Mizuki in the cafeteria. Only Josh could bring himself to make eye contact with her. Later that night, Josh lay in his bunk, and listened to the sound of the massive door sliding shut, and the huge lock engaging. It was done. The troops were locked in, without a single guard inside the building. They had begun locking the doors two days ago, after the cliff murder. They refused to admit murder, but they were taking steps against it. Josh tapped the underside of Alex's bed. Alex dropped to the floor, silently. Josh threw back the covers and stood up. He and Alex looked at each other for a while, brothers in crime.

They were both already wearing stealth suits they had stolen from the training course earlier. Josh had his revolver holstered to his thigh, and Alex's knife at his chest. Alex was unarmed, both men wore masks. They silently made their way through the shadows to the front of the Block. Willam was close behind them, silent as they were. They located Spencer's bed and tapped him on the forehead. He flipped back the covers and silently stood up. Willam met them. He was also dressed in a stolen stealth suit, Spencer was in his pajamas. It was crucial to the plot. the first problem they had to overcome was the lock on the main door of their Block.

Josh knew that the lock was on the other side of the door, only a guard could unlock it. Their original plan was to have Josh shoot his revolver in the bathrooms, then the rest to sneak out the door when the guards came in, but they could not waste a man left behind. They needed all of them. Their new plan was much more devious and clever, but significantly harder to pull off. Josh could barely see Alex and Willam, the suits blended perfectly into the shadows. Alex had taken his position beside the door. Josh crept up to the window and looked out. The street light just outside the block window shone brightly on the two guards standing by the door.

    Josh was looking for one of the three that patrolled around the perimeter of the building. He saw his man. The eldest of the three had just passed. The next one was friends with the two in front of the doors. Josh took the salami out of his pocket, it was juicy and plump. The meat was extremely rare in the camp, and the guards constantly complained of their longing for it. He nodded to Alex, who knocked loudly on the door. The two guards in front of the building spun, looking at the door. Josh took the opportunity to toss the meat. It landed in the middle of the walking path that ran along the front of the building. The guard was sure to notice the rarity.

    "Quiet in there!" The guard at the door yelled. Josh ducked back into the window as the guards turned back around, just as the patrol unit came around the corner. The light from the window illuminated Willam stationed at the window opposite Josh. They were ready.

    "Hey! A salami!" Josh heard the patrol guard exclaim. Josh waited, the next few seconds were crucial.

    "I've got a knife," One of the guards at the door announced, "I'll slice it and we can share." Josh was astounded to hear two sets of footsteps heading toward the path. The door guards had taken the bait. Josh nodded to Willam, and in unison the two yanked the single bar from the window, just as Spencer hammered on the door to cover the noise. Josh had weakened the bars earlier.

"Shut up!" A guard yelled at Spencer. Josh and Willam carefully climbed out the windows, dropping silently to the ground below. They took a long loop around the circle of light, slowly coming up behind the three guards. Willam tossed Josh a rag. In unison they came up behind the two door guards and slapped a hand over their mouths while sliding the syringes into their flesh. The guards bucked sharply in shock, the lorazepam took immediate effect. The third guard put a hand to his mouth to yell for help. Josh was too fast for him.

Josh dropped the unconscious guard to the ground, dashed to the third guard and grabbed him firmly by the wrist. He clasped a hand over his mouth while he spun behind the guard, yanking the guards arm over his shoulder. Josh kicked him in the back of the knees, the guard fell to the ground. He was completely useless. Josh gave a quick yank on the arm, dislocating it. He quickly brought his hand across to the man's neck, jabbing once. The guard immediately crumpled to the the ground, asleep. The salami rolled from his grasp. Josh imitated the call of an eagle, Spencer and Alex dropped from the windows. They were out, and ready to kill.

Josh dragged the three bodies away from the light, into a bush some twenty feet from the Block. Alex had subdued the next patrol guard, and it would be three minutes before the next one came and discovered the door guards missing. They left Willam behind to keep him from sounding the alarm. Josh, Alex, and Spencer made their way through the dark, across the basket ball court, around the fountain, and crouched in a bush thirty feet away from Alexis's Block. They could clearly make out the two guards at the door under the electric light.

The patrol guard came around the corner, and Alex cued Spencer. Spencer, in his pajamas, ran from the bush, screaming like a madman, running straight passed the guards and toward the dining hall. There was some confusion between the guards before the patrol guard was sent after him, the two door guards remained there. There was a gunshot off in the distance. Josh had given Spencer his revolver. It would be confiscated, but Josh could win another in a knife fight. The other two patrol guards soon ran from around the corner, off in Spencer's direction. It was against protocol to wake any other guards for any less than three men. That made Spencer the perfect distraction. For being past curfew he would suffer nothing more than half rations for two weeks. Josh, Alex and Willam would fill in the rest of his food. No harm done.

Willam came up behind them and tapped Josh and Alex on the shoulders. He held up two guard's uniforms. Josh and Alex quickly slipped them on. They went far right, then came running up to the door guards.

"We are patrol guards from Block C, we heard a gunshot?" Josh asked, faking a voice.

"Yeah, you heard one all right!" The guard replied, "But get back to your station. We have this under control." As the man talked Josh and Alex had positioned themselves directly in front of the two guards.

"Okay," Josh replied, as he and Alex punched the two guards in the face. The two men crumpled to the ground. Josh reached down and grabbed their keys, and slid them into the lock. Josh and Alex stripped from their uniforms, back into the stealth suits. Willam quickly came up and began to drag the bodies to a bush. Spencer would have been taken to a holding cell for the rest of the night, one guard would remain with him. When the other two came back, Willam would sedate them. The sedatives would last approximately five hours, more than enough time. Josh and Alex Slowly slid open the door, went into the building, and shut the door behind them.

Josh and Alex crouched together in the shadows. They had to wait an hour, until they were sure that the women in the cabin were asleep. Some may have woken with the commotion. Josh and Alex waited, whispering quietly about who they had been before the camp. They really got to know each other crouched there in the shadows for an hour, but somehow it seemed that Alex only ever told Josh things he had already learned.

    Josh checked his watch. It was time. One hour had past, one hour remaining to the shift change. Willam would have been back in his bed long ago, Spencer asleep in his cell. Josh woke a now sleeping Alex, the two snuck down the rows. They knew where her bed was. She was on the top bunk, the last one in the Block. Nobody slept below her. They managed to make it to the other side of the Block without being spotted. Josh saw her, laying in bed. He signaled Alex to watch the hall, then Josh lay in the bunk under her. It was only fair that he had to kill her, he was her best friend.

    He crouched on the bunk, and slowly reached his hands around the sides of the bunk above. He glanced at Alex's knife open in his right hand. He suddenly brought his left hand down, clamping over her mouth. He stopped his right hand just as the knife touched her neck, not drawing any blood. Something was wrong. Her mouth felt cold, clammy, and wet. Josh brought his hands down, ripped a flashlight from his chest and shone it on his hand. Blood. He stood up, shining the light on Alexis. She was already dead. She had been stabbed in the throat while she slept.

CHAPTER SEVEN

Josh and Alex sprinted across the yard, shaking in fear, cold sweat pouring off their brows. Josh was teary. Suddenly... a flashlight. Alex grabbed Josh and pulled him into a bush just as the light swept over the area. Alex slapped Josh across the face.

"Get it together man! I'm pretty shook up too, but we need to get back to our Block before they find the body!" Alex whispered angrily.

"I don't even really care that she's dead!" Josh exclaimed, "I mean, yeah, I'm sad that she's gone, I'm gonna miss her, and its sad that she's so young, but I don't really care about any of that!"

"Then what are you crying about?" Alex asked.

"She was obviously *murdered*, Alex!" Josh exclaimed.

"So?" Alex asked, "Lots of people have been murdered!"

"But this proves that she's not the killer! We were about to kill an *innocent* person!" Josh whispered back, angrily. The two fell silent, Alex let the news sink in. The two wordlessly decided that they would not tell Spencer or Willam of the development. They would tell them that as she died she had told them she had an accomplice. Josh had almost committed unprovoked, premeditated first degree murder that night. He wasn't worried about getting caught with the guards here, but looking back Josh realized that he had left evidence leading to him all over the place. He wiped her blood from his hands, staining the wet grass.

    Josh and Alex crouched there for a few minutes, before they slowly stood up and sprinted back to their Block. The bars were still out of the windows, and the guards had not been replaced. Josh boosted Alex up into the window. Alex pulled Josh in, they stripped from their stealth suits. They carefully replaced the bars, then snuck back to their bunks. As Josh climbed into his sheets, hearing Alex do the same above him, he thought of how difficult it had been to survive this far in the damned camp, and he wasn't even halfway through.

    Josh was nearly asleep when a terrifying realization hit him. His eyes flew open, he clenched at the sheets and tensed his muscles. It was so simple, Josh had no idea how he had overlooked it. Such a terrifying fact, such a simple fact, one that stood out above all others.

    "Alex," Josh whispered. A faint murmur was the reply. "Alexis... she... she wasn't in the higher grades. She wasn't even in the top ten. It wasn't her turn Alex, the murderer killed her because *we* were planning to. He was sending a message *directly to me.* He's onto us, Alex." The two men were shaken, scared for life. Alexis's murder had really brought the killings home. Josh's circle of friends had always offered a sense of false security. But now one of them had been killed. And none of them were safe.

*   *   *

    Josh looked over at Alex. The mud they had smeared on their faces disguised them against the natural backdrop. It came down to Block A versus Block C again. Josh clutched the assault rifle, Alex his sniper rifle. They were moving along the mountain together. Josh watched Alex's back from ambush while he sniped out enemies below. Willam and

Spencer were leading leading a large group of soldiers through the valley. It was crucial that at least five of those ten soldiers made it to the other side. That was the objective. It was a Block A vs Block C only game, Block A got twenty minutes to prep, then Block C came through. There was a flare on the other side, it required five men to launch.

"Josh, scout a few feet ahead, there's a sniper there. I'll take out those two across the ridge, then when you get back, with that guy's sniper rifle, help me take out that patrol heading for our boys," Alex ordered. Josh nodded, flicking the safety off his rifle, silently moving into the bush. Alex looked down his scope, aiming the rifle across the valley. The men on the other side were good. There was a thin layer of snow on the ground, and the enemy was dressed in snow camouflage they had bought from a guard. Alex was still dressed in his jungle fatigues, a much easier target. He would have to beat them on sniping skill alone. He quickly tightened the silencer, making sure that it was secure. He scanned across the valley at twenty times magnification. He watched carefully, waiting for the enemy to make a mistake. There it was. One of them had moved their rifle, the watery winter sun glinting off his scope.

Alex adjusted slightly, aiming his rifle directly at where the glint came from. He held his breath, steadied the rifle, pulled the bolt, and squeezed the trigger. The small spit resounded in the clearing, Alex watched the bullet fly through the air, straight at the origin of the glint. There was a second shimmer, the man had fallen. Alex moved his rifle a few feet to the right, waiting for the next man to give himself up.

"Come on you bastard!" Alex exclaimed. He was worried that the man had seen his rifle when it recoiled after the shot. He needed to take out that enemy before he was a dead man. Good thing he was the best damn sniper in the camp.

Josh moved slowly through the brush, not making a sound. If the sniper heard him, he would be dead in a second.

He clutched his rifle, slowly pulling back the bolt. He came to the edge of the clearing, and crouched in the bush. He could barely make out the sniper, in full snow camo, laying on the ground. A second man crouched behind him, staring straight at Josh. Josh held his breath. The sentry looked away. He had not seen Josh. Josh pulled the silencer from his tactical belt, and slowly screwed it onto his rifle. He raised the weapon, taking careful aim, not wanting to miss.

Josh squeezed the trigger, sending projectiles flying into the sentry. A small amount of blood spurted from his chest as he crumpled to the ground. The sniper rolled to his feet, turning to face Josh. Josh sprinted out of the bush. The sniper quickly brought the scope to his eye, squeezing off a round. The bullet ricocheted off of Josh's rifle, forcing him to drop it. Josh could not believe his luck. He was upon the sniper, tackling him to the ground. Josh punched the man in the face, who immediately went limp. Josh grabbed his own rifle, and the sniper rifle, and made his way back to Alex.

The two men lay in the clearing, scopes to their eyes. They were waiting for the go from the ground troop. They had their crosshairs trained on two men in the ambush group, they would be the first down.

"Ground patrol, you are nearing the ambush group, do we have the clear to fire?" Alex asked into his radio. Despite his wild, rebellious exterior, when it came to sniping he was nothing but professional.

"Hold fire, overwatch one, we will take up offensive positions," Spencer replied. Josh saw the men on the ground fan out, taking cover behind boulders and overturned barrels. "Copy, on your mark," Spencer radioed back. Alex opened fire, the man on the ground flying backward, landing hard on the ground. Josh squeezed off a round, nicking the man he was aiming at, causing him to clutch at his shoulder. Josh quickly pulled the bolt, took aim again, and finished the poor bastard off. He was nowhere near as good as Alex.

"You try to run..." Alex whispered to himself, he squeezed the trigger and a man running toward ground patrol fell, "I shoot you in the face. You try to hide behind a boulder," Alex pulled the bolt and scoped the man, he shot, "I shoot you in the face. You shoot one of our boys... I shoot you in the face," Another man fell, "You begin to call a retreat..." Alex continued, headshotting the leader of the ambush force, "I shoot you in the face." Josh finished off the rest of the team while Alex took out the main players.

"All clear ground patrol, move forward cautiously, you're down to five men, and your a quarter click out from the launch station," Josh reported into his mic.

"Copy, give us overwatch, now more than ever," Willam replied. Josh looked down to see an enemy crawling along the ground, pistol drawn.

"Alex!" Josh called, pointing to the man. Alex pulled the bolt, aimed, and shot. *Click.* Alex dropped the mag and pulled a second from his belt, swearing at himself. Josh was out of ammunition as well. Alex shoved the second mag into his rifle, pulled the bolt, and scoped, quickly. The bastard on the ground took a shot, taking out one of the C Block ground patrol, milliseconds before Alex's shot hit him in the throat.

"Dammit!" Alex yelled, a sweat breaking out, his pupils dilated. Josh had seen it once before from him. He was on the verge of a breakdown. The were down to four men on the ground.

"Alex! Calm down!" Josh yelled at him, slapping him across the face. Alex looked at Josh, stunned. "The ridge we are standing on gradually slants downward, coming to a mere twenty feet above the ground at the launch station. We continue along this way, give them overwatch, then at the end we drop down and give them a hand with the launch! Easy!" Josh explained. Alex smiled at him, happy with the explanation. Alex grabbed at the radio on his shoulder, flicking it on.

"Come in ground patrol! All is not lost, move forward as planned, we have a scheme, repeat, move forward as planned!" Alex called into the mic.

"Copy Alex," Willam's voice came over the radio.

"Who went down?" Alex asked, when suddenly commotion stirred in the clearing. Bullets ripped through the greenery, shattering the silence, breaking the peace. Josh hit the ground immediately, crawling behind a fallen log. Josh looked up to see three consecutive bullets blast their way into Alex's chest. He hit the ground, out of the game.

"Damn it all to hell!" Josh yelled over the sound of the massive gun across the valley. Josh knew that he needed to take it out before it turned its attention to the ground force. Josh pulled the sniper rifle off his back, pulled the bolt, and said a prayer to the God he didn't believe in. If only he had learned how to snipe faster. He was rubbish at it. Josh slowly looked around the side of the log, sticking the end of his barrel out. He looked down the scope, he quickly sighted the muzzle flashes across the valley. It was a large gatling gun, and the gunner was well armored. Josh increased the magnification on the scope.

There was a tiny slit in the armor plate of which the gunner looked through, aiming the weapon. Josh placed the crosshairs carefully aligned at the slot, dead on the gunner's head. The wood of the log was being ripped apart, and soon a bullet would find it's way through to Josh. Josh took the shot. He watched the bullet bounce off the turret's protective plating. Josh pulled back behind the log. As he reset the weapon, he remembered Alex's words from the week before: "A good sniper doesn't always shoot to kill. Occasionally he shoots to distract, or even get himself detected."

Josh took a pair of binoculars from his tactical vest and once again he looked at the turret. There was the main gun, two small metal plates stuck vertically in the ground, no doubt for support teams to take cover behind, the ammunition belt piled on the ground, and... there was Josh's opening. A barrel of the toxin in Josh's grenades stood beside the turret, probably to give an advantage to the poor bastard on the business end of the large gun. Josh thanked the sky for this opportunity, then carefully came around the side of the log again.

    Josh looked down the scope, this time aiming at the pressurized barrel. The bullets stopped flying into the clearing... the gun was beginning to sweep downward, about the take out the ground team. Josh placed his crosshairs over the barrel, held his breath as Alex did, and squeezed the trigger. The un-silenced shot resounded in the valley, the bullet directly penetrating the barrel. The green gas sprayed from the barrel, forced out by its own density. The man at the turret abandoned his post, running from the gas. He passed out on the ground seconds later. Josh saw men emerge from behind the walls, running from the barrel. Only one made it out 'alive'. The turret was officially out of operation.

    Josh went over to Alex, he was breathing slightly, twitching every now and then. Josh placed a hand on his forehead, he was cold. Josh closed the man's eyes, saluted the body, then took off.

    Josh sprinted along the ridge, the ground team had made substantial progress while he was dealing with the turret. He came to their position. From there it was a straight shot to the station. Josh knew that a great force would be awaiting the C Block men just over the hill in front of them. Josh sprinted past the ground team, coming parallel with the crest of the hill in the valley. What he saw confirmed his worst fears.

    Half of A Block, roughly fifty men, were positioned on the other side of the hill, waiting to ambush the C Block team. Josh knew what he had to do. He reported the situation to Willam over the radio, lay on the ground, and shouldered his rifle. He screwed Alex's silencer onto the barrel. Not being detected would be crucial in the next few moments. Josh noticed that about ten of the men straggled behind the rest of the group, nobody would notice them go down. Josh took them out first, very careful not to miss a single shot. Then Josh's plan came into action.

He ramped up the magnification on the scope so he could make out every detail of every man's uniform. He looked toward the center of the enemy team, and found a good mark. The grenades on the man's belt were very prominent. Josh unscrewed the silencer. He lined the crosshairs at the grenade, checked for wind, and adjusted his aim. He had to make this shot, or the game was lost.

"At the gunshot, you charge the hill, copy?" Josh asked into the mic.

"Copy," Spencer's voice came back. There was an eerie quiet across the valley. The calm before the storm. Josh held his breath, double checked his aim, and squeezed the trigger. Almost in slow motion Josh watched the bullet fly through the air, straight and true, directly striking the grenade on the man's belt. The explosive went off, the green fog blanketing nearly half the enemy force. C Block followed through with their plan, the volley of grenades flew over the hill, exploding in the midst of the chaos ensuing on the enemy side. Josh eyed the cliff in front of him, roughly fifty feet down.

He watched the C Block team charge the hill, opening fire on the bewildered opponents, grabbing cover before A Block had time to return fire. Josh dropped the sniper rifle, throwing caution to the wind. He slid off the edge of the cliff, zooming down at a barely controlled speed. He hit the snow bank at the bottom heavily, plummeting through the powder, hitting the ground beneath hard. A cut on his arm was bleeding bad, staining the white snow red. Josh began to freeze, it was unbelievably cold under the snow and ice. The gunfire and explosions above were muffled by the powder.

Josh began to claw his way out. He needed to help his Block mates. A hand broke through the cover of snow, reaching down for Josh. He grasped it, and was pulled upward. He emerged into the world of battle, a cacophony of vociferous bangs and loud noises, the screams of men and the flashes of guns. He looked up into Spencer's eyes. His face was streaked with blood. Willam was there too, the three men were crouched behind an overturned truck.

"We haven't lost anybody yet!" Willam informed Josh.

"How many enemies left?" Josh asked.

"Roughly twenty, Josh. We're outnumbered four to one!" Spencer moaned.

"Get it together, Eberstark! If you can't handle the war, I'll take you out right now. But if you can, get out there and save some lives!" Josh yelled. Spencer nodded, cocking his rifle. He screamed as he ran from the cover of the truck, bullets whizzing by him before he dove to the ground behind a pile of empty barrels.

"Spencer, Give us a mark!" Willam yelled, readying his rifle. Josh loaded his. Spencer peeked around the side of the barrel, then whipped his head back in.

"Two rogues five feet apart, fifteen feet ahead of you, two to your right!" He yelled back over the sounds of battle. Josh looked at Willam, and Willam at Josh. They were both thinking of the same strategy. Josh whipped around the right side of the truck as Willam whipped around the left, they opened fire on the two targets, for roughly five seconds, before pulling back behind cover.

"They're out!" Willam confirmed. Josh swept around and fired at a few more enemies, bullets sparking and ricocheting off the vehicle beside him, burying themselves in the ground. Josh flinched as a bullet broke through the metal, whizzing very near his ear. He flung around the side, pulling the trigger, the bolt flying back and forward as bullets poured from the barrel, letting out an ear shattering bang. Josh pulled back behind the car, an enemy focused fire on where he had been seconds before. Josh pulled a grenade from his belt and tossed it over the car. He heard a scream, then a bang.

Josh dropped the clip from his rifle and shoved another in it's place. It was his last clip. He pulled the bolt back, screamed, and dove from cover, sprinting toward the enemy, bullets whizzing past him. He dove for a small wooden wall as a bullet ripped through the flesh on his left arm, skimming through a thin tear of skin, blasting out the other side of his arm, bringing a stream of dark red blood with it. Josh fell to the ground, dropping his rifle, clutching at his arm, blood seeping through his fingers. It was not a deep cut, but the projectile had severed a vein. Josh clenched his teeth in pain. He quickly took off his boot, pulled off his sock and shoved his boot back on, quickly retying it with one hand.

Josh tied the sock around his wound, the grey fabric instantly stained red. He wondered if enough of the tranquilizer had made it into his bloodstream to take him out. After he retrieved his rifle from the mud he scuttling back behind the cover. Willam came up, diving to the ground beside him.

"Josh, we're winning! We've taken no fatalities, and they are down to fifteen soldiers!" Willam yelled at Josh. Josh couldn't hear anything but a loud buzzing noise, his vision was blurred and he felt extremely tired. His movements were sluggish. He had taken enough tranquilizer, he was going down soon. "Josh?" Willam asked. Suddenly it all zoomed back. Josh could see again, his hearing returned.

"What?" Josh asked.

"They're retreating!" Spencer yelled from somewhere behind Josh. It was true. The men were turning and running. Some of the C Block guys shot them in the backs as they ran, the A Block men fell into the dirt. Josh stood, unleashing his gun into the mob of retreating men. By the time the C Block soldiers had run over a hill in the distance they were down to seven men. Josh and the other four men made their way forward, sprinting toward the launch station.

It was a large, metal cylinder with buttons every two feet. Four of the men ran up and held down their buttons, looking back for Josh. His breath had become labored, he was limping slowly, his vision blurred, his hearing gone. He came to the cylinder as he fell to his knees, crawling forward. He reached up a hand. Suddenly a bullet ricocheted off the cylinder, the A Block soldiers had returned, attacking when they were most vulnerable. With his last ditch of effort, Josh threw his weight upward, slammed his hand down on the button, then collapsed on the ground, passing out.

CHAPTER EIGHT

"Josh! Josh! Josh, where the hell are you?" Alex called, running through Block C. He hadn't found him in the Block, in the yard, in the canteen, anywhere. He found Spencer, he had no idea where he was either. Willam was at the shooting range, too focused to reply. Alex started to look under Josh's bunk, but then realized that that would be ridiculous. Suddenly he heard Josh's voice, calling his name, from the front of the Block. Alex turned and ran, Josh ran as well. Alex turned the corner and they smacked into each other, tumbling to the ground.

"Finals today!" Both men yelled at each other in unison. The way the camp was set, you only take half your classes in the beginning of the year, then finals, then another set of courses, then another set of finals. Josh and Alex sprinted out of the building. They shared the first class, military strategy. They came into the lecture hall with one minute to spare, their professor instructed them to sit immediately. The professor brought them their supplies, a pencil, two pens, an eraser, and a calculator. Their test was handed out. It must have been forty pages thick. The board said they had two hours.

Josh immediately dove into the test, quickly answering the questions in the small test booklet, rushing through without checking an answer. The questions were a good mix of history, active decisions, theoretical situations, and moral dilemmas. Josh was good in this subject, he had a cold, calculating mind, which is what was needed to be an efficient strategist. Alex sat to Josh's left, clearly dumbfounded. He whispered quietly to Josh.

"Dude, I can't get past question five!" Alex hurriedly got across as another student sneezed. Josh pulled a stack of sticky notes from his pocket, jotted down the answers from five to fifteen on a note and stuck it to the bottom of his boot. He then put his leg up on his knee, the note clearly visible to Alex. Alex began to quickly answer the questions, stealing Josh's answers. The professor walked behind Josh, who casually put his leg back down. The answers were hidden. When the professor made a round in another section of the study hall, Josh put his leg up again, Alex took down the rest of the notes. Josh was nearly halfway done with the test when Alex pestered him again.

"I can't get fifty six!" Alex whispered as a student was asking a question. Josh couldn't use the post it note again, it would seem too suspicious. He looked around the room, scanning for another option. He found his entry. He signed to Alex to throw his eraser out the nearby open window while the professor had his back turned. Alex tossed the eraser, and Josh quickly wrote down the next few answers along the tip of his eraser. He handed in the eraser to Alex in full view of the professor.

"Hey!" The old man yelled, "No cheating!" He screamed.

"Sir, I'm just passing him an eraser. You didn't hand him one in the beginning of class," Josh explained. The old man frowned at them, then turned away, accepting the ruse. Josh finished handing the eraser to Alex. Alex eyed the answers on the end of the eraser, then copied them into his notes. Fifty six, B. Fifty seven, C. Fifty eight, B. Fifty nine, E. Sixty, A. Alex grinned as he rubbed the eraser across his paper, wiping the answers from the tip. The two grinned at each other, then went back to writing the test. The end was called just as Josh wrote the last sentence of his essay. He looked over, Alex was just writing the first of his.

"Dude, I flunked that thing!" Alex screamed as the two exited the building, he grabbed at his now thick hair.

"All the answers I gave you were correct, bro. You're gonna lose twenty marks for the essay, saying you got ninety on the rest of the test, thats seventy... your class average before that was an... eighty three? That means know you've got a... seventy seven. Hey, that's still passing!" Josh tried to cheer Alex up.

"What's my overall average now?" Alex asked.

"You have one hundred in all the weapons based classes, and eighty two average in all the other classes, ninety four in the battle marks, your overall average... eighty seven," Josh replied.

"Shit! God, I almost hope that psychopath kills everybody! I need to be in the group that gets chosen!" Alex screamed, spinning in a circle.

"Hey... that's not cool. That horrible excuse for a man killed one of our friends," Josh said sternly to Alex. "But why do you even need to get in the chosen group anyway? It's just going to work for some secret agency. With your skills, you could climb the ranks of the military like a ladder!" Josh exclaimed.

"Because I can't afford to not make it in!" Alex exclaimed, "They said that if I didn't get into the agency, I would go back to prison. I burned some bridges there when I left man... If I don't get into the agency... I'm going to end up with being somebodies girlfriend... and... and a long thin strip of razor in my gut!"

"Oh... I'm sorry too... yikes," Josh replied, taken aback. The two slowly walked around the yard, making their way to the next exam. Finally Josh broke the awkward silence.

"What did you even do to go to jail in the first place?" Josh asked, hoping that Alex would finally spill his secrets in his moment of weakness.

"I..." Alex started, as if searching for the words. "I used to cook, Josh."

"What do you-"

"Meth, Josh. I used to cook meth. And I was damn good at it too. Ninety nine point seven purity. I was bringing in roughly a hundred thousand bucks a month. I had four guys working for me, I had a huge lab set up in my basement. Don't take me wrong Josh, I never touched the stuff. In fact, I spent most of the money on my friends and family, I was just in it for the thrill. The excitement of evading the law, breaking it.

"I used to deal to this big distributer named Big Danny. He took all my product and sold it to the addicts and the like. One day, I messed up. Cheating the police and the DEA wasn't enough. I started cutting my meth, seeing if I could slip it by Danny, just for one deal. I brought in double my average dosage, and he payed me double. I turned to leave when he tested it, and discovered my ruse. Him and his two bodyguards opened fire on me with assault rifles. Imagine that, killing a seventeen year old kid, an orphan on the streets! That was the first time I picked up a sniper rifle, Josh. I took it out of their trunk as I took cover behind their car. I felt an instant connection. It was beautiful. I stood from behind the car, quickly bringing the scope to my eye and taking a shot. The first man fell. Then the second, I shot Danny in the leg. I walked over to him, placed the barrel against his face, and took the shot. I dropped the rifle and left.

"The cops took my prints off the gun, and traced them to me. They raided my house and found my lab. I was taken to court, tried for possession of narcotics, cooking, and the triple murder. I was immediately sentenced to life. Then some God-sent guard found me at the shooting range, taking my amazing shots. He had a cousin in the I.E.M.F, and recommended me for 'Special Bail.' That was my eighteenth birthday. Two months later, I was sent here. Then I met you. And you know the rest. Josh, when I left that prison, I gave a speech that would make you punch me down right now. About how every man there was a bastard, and how they didn't deserve to be alive. Then I left. If I go back there, I'm a dead man," Alex finished his riveting tale. Josh was stunned. They had come to their next building. They shook hands good luck, and entered together.

*   *   *

TWO DAYS LATER

"All right, privates, up on your feet!" The General called from the podium in the center of the gigantic room. The mass of men and women stood, Josh, Spencer, Willam and Alex among them. There was an empty seat next to Josh, where Alexis should have sat. "Now, you have officially come half way through your time here at Camp Razor's Edge!" The General called. A cheer came up from the audience. "The Master is here to give you all a speech. On the way out of the meeting, you will be given your new schedules. I am sorry to say that a great number of you failed your exams..." Josh saw Alex tense at this, "And a few of you aced all of them. We will also post the new leader board tomorrow night."

"You're posting a death sentence," Josh whispered under his breath. Somewhere in that room, the bastard that had killed so many smirked.

"And now, your lord and leader, The Master!" The General called triumphantly. The students cheered, mandatorily, as the man in flowing red robes and his private guards entered the room, sweeping across the floor and taking the podium.

"Troops of this glorious camp..." He began. The men and women sat again. Josh and Alex zoned out. All the important information had already been told to them, this was just a propaganda speech to keep moral up.

"We need to take down that list the second it's posted," Josh whispered to Alex.

"Agreed. We can't let the psychopath see it, he'll get his next targets," Alex replied quietly.

"Or perhaps... and I'm just putting this out there..." Willam interjected, "We do let the murderer see the list. If he or she's first, then the killing will stop!" Willam offered. The three thought about this for a minute.

"No... the odds are against it," Josh replied finally.

"I agree. There is a much better chance of us giving out names than thwarting the guy..." Alex agreed.

"Yeah, I guess you guys are right. But... there will be guards there when it's posted, how will we take it down?" Willam asked.

"Good point, again. Perhaps we must take a more passive approach. Besides, they could just put another list up. I think we should survey the area closely, see if anybody takes too close a look, or writes down any names..." Josh theorized. The other two nodded. Suddenly something The Master said caught Josh's ear. He shushed the other two.

"And any rumors you hear of homicide drifting around camp, you can toss from your minds. There has, I admit, been a suspicious string of suicides and unfortunate accidents, but they are nothing more than that. The guards have looked into each event, and assure you that they are not murders. I urge you to report anybody you hear saying otherwise to one of your beloved guards. Now... off to bed with you! You will all find a halfway present on your bunks. Goodnight!" The Master finished, as the troops stood he turned and exited the building.

"Gift? What do you think it could be? Something to torture us more?" Spencer asked sarcastically as they filed out of the building.

"Yeah, maybe a steel wool sweater, God knows its cold out here," Alex retorted.

"Josh, everybody wants that trench coat you bought. I heard tell that somebody was planning to shiv you for it!" Willam exclaimed.

"Rumors and hogwash. Better report it to one of our 'Beloved Guards'. God, I hate that 'The Master', he's just a puppet to take hate for The General. Anybody here read 1984? There's your big brother!" Josh ranted, snow crunching under his boots. He snugged the coat around his shoulders.

"Hello, boys!" Mizuki called from a distance to Josh's right. Josh and Alex turned together.

"Hello, Mizuki!" They said in unison. Behind their backs, Willam and Spencer mocked them. She bounced up to them, giddy as ever.

"Did you guys know that one week today is Christmas on the outside?" She asked. The men were shocked. They had completely forgotten that holidays existed.

"I... had no idea..." Josh began, amazed that he had forgotten such a major event in his childhood. Back at the orphanage, Ace had made a promise. He would be there every Christmas, with some form of contraband, to cheer up Josh's whole year. Josh suddenly felt sad at the fact that this would be the first Christmas in six years that Ace wouldn't be there.

"Josh, I have absolutely nothing to get you!" Alex exclaimed sarcastically. Josh noticed Mizuki shaking in the cold. A thin layer of fresh snow lined her shoulders. Josh slid off his trench coat and gave it to her, the cold hit him like a stone.

"Josh... I couldn't! You'll die without it!" She exclaimed.

"I insist. Consider it an early Christmas present," Josh replied, forcing the coat into her hands. She slipped it on, and visibly relaxed in the warm. Josh looked over his shoulder at Alex, and smirked. He thought of when he and Mizuki had kissed in the hospital, and wondered what it meant.

"Well, we should get back to our Block before we're beaten there!" Alex laughed, trying to pry Josh from the tender moment with Mizuki. Josh waved goodbye, turned on his heel, and trudged back to the Block with his friends.

"Score one Stone!" Spencer laughed. Alex turned and shoved him into the snow playfully. Spencer got up and went to shove Alex lightly. Suddenly Alex spun and punched Spencer, hard. He fell to the ground, bleeding. Alex descended on him, punching him over and over again. Blood sprayed everywhere. Spencer went limp, Alex kept punching him.

Josh came out of his vision and shook off the possibility, holding Spencer back from shoving Alex. Josh shook his head at him. Alex was hurt that Josh was making more progress than him. The four men entered the Block, they were the last ones in. The guards slid the door closed behind them, locking it. There was commotion in the Block, the men ecstatic about the gifts. Josh shielded his eyes, he wanted to be surprised. Spencer split off to his bunk, Alex and Josh to theirs, Willam continued on to his bunk. Josh found two packages on his bed. One the signature wrapping of the Camp, the other was blue wrapping paper with black graduation hats on it.

Josh dove into the camp one first. It contained, thank god, a fresh pair of pajamas, softer that Josh's original pair. He quickly changed into them, on the spot. The package also contained a small chocolate bar. Josh took a bite of this and immediately realized how much he had missed sugar. There were no sweets at the camp. Also in the package there was a pack of cigarettes, which Josh would sell to a guard, there was a warm sweater, and a new pillow. Josh was amazed by this. It was softer than the pillows they had at the orphanage.

It was actually unbelievable. Josh then moved to the second, smaller package.

Josh ripped into it, and what met his eyes was beautiful. There was a picture of he and Ace, taken five months before he had left for the camp. There was also a small mirror. Josh looked in the mirror next to the picture. He looked much harder, older, more mature. Josh had tears in his eyes. He missed his old mentor so much. Also in the package was a thick book. The Lord of the Rings trilogy, Josh had been dying to read, and Ace knew that this was his favorite series. There was a card stuck in the book, Josh pulled it out and flipped it open. He immediately recognized the handwriting as Ace's. Josh quickly read the letter.

Josh, I have been told by my brother that you are still alive, and one of the healthier 'subjects' as he referred to you. I am so proud, Josh. You deserve the book, I know they haven't given any to you, what hell. My brother also informed me that you are 'conspiring' about murders officially labeled as suicides. Josh, I just want you to know that I believe you, and that you should follow the investigation closely. There could be danger for you if this serial killer continues. I can't write much longer, I'm being deployed in three minutes, but I got your grades. You are holding a ninety seven point eight, you are third of your class! Amazing job, Josh... I really...

Josh went back and read again. *You are third of your class!* Suddenly the world fell apart around Josh. Ace had been right. He was in danger. In fact, he was third to next on the killer's list. Josh felt sick. He fell to his bed, nearly vomiting. Somebody out there wanted to kill him. Not out of defense... or out of necessity. For *fun*. Somebody wanted to kill him for *sport*. Josh dropped the card and sprinted to the bathroom, puking into the toilet. He had never experienced such a strange combination of terror and disgust. He had to catch the killer, and he only had two kills more of evidence to do it. Josh fell to his knees. it seemed hopeless.

Alex came into the bathroom, and helped Josh to his feet.

"What happened, man?" Alex asked.

"I'm third in the class..." Josh replied, monotone.

"Good for you!" Alex exclaimed. Then his face blanked, he paled. "But that means... oh God, Josh, I'm so sorry. I'll stand by you day and night. I will guard you with my life until you catch this son of a bitch."

"Thanks, Alex," Josh replied, making his way back to his bunk. "Let the other two know, I need sleep. I'll let you sleep tonight... the list has not been posted... the killer will not know it yet. God, this is... bad."

ONE WEEK LATER

"Merry Christmas Josh!" Alex called, pulling on his friend's foot to wake him up. Josh stirred, slowly waking up. Alex was crouching over him, it startled Josh. Josh pushed Alex off his bed. He checked the watch he had bought from a guard.

"Ten 'o'clock?" Josh asked, jumping from the bed, diving for his clothes.

"Relax, mate!" Willam called from across the room, running up to Josh.

"Yeah, it appears that the bastards do have hearts after all!" Spencer came up behind Willam.

"Why are you guys still in your pajamas? Why aren't you at class?" Josh asked, pulling off his shirt, grabbing his military fatigues off the nightstand.

"Keep your shirt on, Josh! They gave us the day off!" Alex whistled, basking in the freedom. They didn't even get weekends at the camp

"What?" Josh asked, stunned.

"Yeah, the whole day, to us!" Willam was bursting. Josh slipped back into his pajama top. He dove under his bed, coming up with an armful of small parcels.

"I managed to bribe the guards to get something for all of you..." Josh explained, handing out the parcels. The men accepted them graciously. Spencer ripped into his first. Josh had bought him the complete set of Bourne novels.

"Now you don't have to read that soldier's scribbles anymore..." Josh explained.

"Thank you so much Josh, they were starting to get repetitive..." Spencer laughed, grinning at the gift.

"You better like it! It was damned hard to get these!" Josh replied. Spencer tucked the books under his arm. Willam opened his next.

"Now, Willam, even though we hang out all the time, I feel like I don't know any of your hobbies or even what you used to do before camp, but I think this fits you..." Josh explained. Willam finished opening the package. Inside was a fine black suit, complete with tie and shoes.

"Josh, I love it. I have felt that the uniform here is a little informal. *Heh*, no more casual clothes for me!" Willam ran off to change into the fabric. Josh grinned, he knew that Willam was a suit.

"And Alex, this is the best thing I could think to get you. I had a guard talk to Ace, and it was put into development immediately. I measured your eye socket while you were asleep... this is entirely for you," Josh said warmly to his closest friend. Alex ripped open the paper, and blew out his breath, taken aback. He sat on the bed, cradling the item like a baby.

"Well... what is it?" Spencer asked. Alex slowly pulled the scope out of the paper, handling it delicately. It was long, sleek and black.

"You can side lenses in or out of the main chamber, switching between four, six, ten, fifteen, twenty, and twenty five times zoom. Switches between five different crosshair designs, and three reticle designs. Auto calibrates upon switches of magnification, mounts to Picatinny, Weaver, and four other kinds of rail I've never even heard of... rotates on the mount to match your shooting style, and as I said, perfectly fit to your eye socket. Also heat and frost resistant, perfect for any environment," Josh gave Alex the specs. Josh pulled a small black case from under his bed and handed it to Alex, "The case is made for the scope. The metal of the scope and the case are both bullet proof, reinforced glass on the front and back lenses, can take pressure of up to one hundred and fifty pounds. Both pieces are nearly indestructible."

"Josh... I..." Alex stammered, admiring the scope.

"Currently you are the only man on earth with this exact scope. But, its so versatile, the agency is going to start making it a standard. Its name... the A-L3-X," Josh smirked at the clever name. Alex jumped from the bed, throwing his arms around Josh, hugging him tightly.

"Josh... this is the best gift anybody has ever given me. In my life. Thank you so much," Alex held his friend out at arm's length, examining him. The two smiled at each other. "Now, my gift to you... I met with The General two days ago, and after some serious arguing... well, It's better that you-"

"Stone! Report!" A voice screamed from the front of the Block. Josh pulled on his casual clothes quickly, and began for the front of the Block.

"Wait, Josh!" Spencer called. Josh turned. Spencer threw Josh a light black leather jacket with a permanently up collar, "Merry Christmas." Josh smiled at Spencer, slipped on the coat, then turned and ran to the front of the block. The General stood there. Josh wondered if it had anything to do with Alex's gift, or if he was in trouble for some reason. He followed The General back to his office. The General left him there alone, sitting in front of the large desk. Suddenly the door flung open. Josh stood out of habit, turning to face the door. He was struck, he could not believe who he saw there. Josh fell back into the chair as the man came into the room.

"Merry Christmas, Josh," Ace smiled, holding out his arms. Josh ran to him, they embraced, a tear streamed down Josh's face. They hugged for a long time before they broke apart. Josh examined Ace, and Ace Josh.

"Ace, you don't have a single wound!" Josh exclaimed. It was so unusual.

"I've been off for two months, but you Josh! You look so much older, so much more mature!" Ace exclaimed. The two exited the office, Ace's arm on Josh's shoulders. The General stood outside his office, frowning in disapproval at his brother. Ace frowned back, watching him like a cat as he and Josh left the building.

"Not very brotherly," Josh commented.

"You know that scum is my brother?" Ace asked. Josh nodded. Them came back to Josh's Block. Josh introduced Ace to his friends. They all seemed surprised at his age. Josh showed Ace where he was living and the meager possessions he owned.

"You want to know something funny, Josh?" Ace asked, chuckling to himself, "This is the exact same bunk that I stayed in while I was here." Ace chuckled to himself, shaking off the coincidence. Josh had never considered that Ace had also attended the camp. Ace and Josh went for a long walk, each talking about what had occurred since Josh had been sent to the camp. Josh pointed out Mizuki to Ace.

"Not bad, Josh. I'd hit it," Ace smirked. They both laughed. At the end of the walk Ace produced a large black box. Josh assumed it was an assault rifle and unclipped the latches. He pulled open the big box and was taken by surprise. He was looking at an acoustic guitar.

"I remember you used to play... assumed you missed feeling the strings. This is the same guitar that was at the orphanage. The same one that Mason had stolen for you," Ace explained, Josh smirked at this, "I also got you ten changes of strings, and fifty picks. Just do me a favor, no stairway to heaven."

"I'll try to suppress it," Josh smirked, pulling the guitar out of the case and straddling it on his knee. He ripped off a Led Zeppelin riff, without missing a note.

"Seems you've still got it," Ace chuckled.

"I'm a little in disrepair," Josh replied, strumming a few chords. The day was drawing to an end. At five o'clock, Ace had to leave. A Blackhawk helicopter descended into the yard, drawing a crowd.

"Why the helicopter?" Josh asked Ace.

"I'm being deployed. Now," Ace replied.

"Hey, don't die on me, okay? I want your face to be the first thing I see when I get out of here," Josh replied. Alex watched the two hug from a distance. He saw Ace whisper something in Josh's ear, which caused Josh to tear up. Ace climbed into the helicopter, Josh saluted him as he flew away. He walked back to the Block with Alex.

"What did he whisper to you?" Alex asked.

"He told me not to get killed, and if I did, he would take out the psychopath that did it," Josh replied. Later that night they sat down to a massive feast in the dining hall. There was much rejoicing. Josh had mulled Ace's last words around all day, something about them seemed... *Ominous.*

CHAPTER NINE

"Josh!" Alex called from across the Block. Josh looked up from his guitar. Willam, Spencer, and Mizuki were woken from their musical trance. Josh stood up as his friend arrived.

"What is it?" Josh asked. The panicked expression on Alex's face worried him.

"I just saw some guards posting the list... I *just* saw them... We need to move now," Alex reported. Josh threw the guitar back on his bed, turning to follow Alex out of the building. Josh looked back to try and explain to Mizuki.

"Just go!" She yelled, shooing him away. Willam and Spencer joined them in the race to the wall. There was already a large crowd of students around the bulletin board.

"We may have missed our opportunity..." Alex panted.

"Shit! Keep a lookout none the less. He may not have seen it yet," Josh commanded. The boys made their way to the front of the crowd, turning back to watch the busy students. Josh saw a knife out of the corner of his eye, he assumed it was one of his visions. He was wrong. Suddenly there were screams. Some ten students had pulled knives, stabbing the man or woman standing next to them. Blood spread into the cobblestone as bodies fell, and students fled. The knife wielding troops looked at each other in confusion for a second, then began to kill each other off. Josh tried to intervene but was shoved back by a guard running to help.

The guards definition of help was to unleash their weapon upon the homicidal maniacs and any unarmed students trapped in the mix. Josh saw Spencer fall.

"Spencer!" Josh called as his friend hit the concrete. The gunfire ceased, the crowd was entirely downed, twitching in a seeping puddle of liquid mortality. Josh rushed forward, grabbed hold of Spencer's face and tried to keep him awake.

"Come on, Spencer!" Josh called, holding his eyelids open. Josh noticed a large knife gash across his friend's midsection. Spencer had been one of the targets. Josh quickly glanced at the list. He was number four. Josh also recognized two and one in the group of the dead. Josh was three. There was seven... five and eight... this was an attack orchestrated by the maniacal bastard behind the other murders. Suddenly Josh saw it all in his mind's eye. A shadowy figure paying off the ten students to stab the top ten on the list, also giving them a target within the group so that they could tie off their own ends. It was a work of pure genius. The psychopath could expunge a great number of his targets without leaving anybody who knew it was him.

Josh felt Spencer go limp in his arms. Josh reached up a blood soaked hand and felt Spencer's pulse. Thank God he was still alive.

"Medic!" Willam yelled from behind Josh. Josh felt himself get ripped from Spencer's body, two nurses rushing forward with a stretcher. The men lifted Spencer and quickly wheeled him in the direction of the hospital. Alex rushed forward and held Josh, who was clearly in shock at being covered in his friend's blood. Josh was shaken, not at the blood, but at one resolute fact. The murderer was not only smart, but *not* a psychopath. A psychopath would have wanted to kill every target individually, enjoying their pain and suffering. But no, he was only driven by the final goal. And he would do anything to get there. Josh shuddered. Why had he survived? The attack had hit the top ten, but he was three... why not him? Josh's ears were ringing, his vision distorted around the edges. His mind was on overload, cycling through every face in the camp, every reason why he was spared... was it just bad planning? No, the killer was too good for that... But who was it?

"Josh... let's go get you washed up..." Willam suddenly said from behind Josh, clasping a hand on Josh's shoulder. The world rushed back to Josh, the sounds of screams and shouts, the feeling of William's hand on his shoulder, the sight of red snow all around him. Willam and Alex led Josh back to the Block, and stuck him in the showers, fully clothed. Josh let the warm water run over him, watching the red stained liquid flow into the drain under him. He fell back against the wall, and slid down, curling his knees up against his chest. He began to cry, tears mixing with blood and water. For the first time in his life, he felt that this was a challenge he could not surmount... an enemy who's wit he could not match...

Josh emerged from the shower some time later, a towel over his shoulders. Alex and Willam were sitting on Josh's bunk, fiddling with Alex's scope. The two stood as Josh came to them, they respected him for what he had been through. Josh just laid on his bunk, picked up his guitar, and began to strum chords at random. Willam and Alex stood, Josh heard PTSD whispered as they walked away. Josh fell asleep at some point, and woke up to the smell of bacon. Willam stood next to the bed, a plate he had stolen from the cafeteria in his hand. Josh sat up, pushing the guitar off him, accepting the plate graciously. He found it hard to eat, but finished it out of respect for Willam.

Josh wandered down to the shooting range some time later, picked up a sniper rifle, just for the heck of it, and put his eye to the scope. He would be penalized for skipping classes that day, but he did not care. Josh picked a target and pulled the trigger, not even caring. He was amazed to see that he hit a direct headshot. Josh couldn't believe it. He pulled the bolt, picked a new target, and fired. Headshot. Josh challenged himself. He picked a moving target, pulled the bolt, and shot. Headshot. Josh threw the rifle down, amazed. Somehow, in the depth of his despair, he found the skill he needed to fire the rifle correctly.

"Not bad, Josh," Alex finally spoke from behind. Josh jumped, he had thought he was alone.

"Thanks, Alex," Josh replied humbly.

"But don't get too cocky. This is nothing compared to out on the real field. Offense and defense at the same time... there's just... there's just nothing like it..." Alex finished, going off into a trance. He snapped back.

"Won't you get in trouble for skipping classes?" Josh asked.

"I was near the epicenter of the attack, I think I will be excused," Alex laughed, "Plus, the curve ain't that bad now." And with that comment it hit Josh. He realized the scariest, but most hopeful fact of all. The killer must have...

"Given the targets to his..." *Men before the attack, therefore he must* "have known the rankings before..." *They were posted, but so did I, therefore...* "We're equals!" Josh exclaimed. Alex had only heard half of the thought process, but understood fully.

"Josh, are we gonna get this guy?" Alex asked, grinning at his friends sudden recovery.

"Alex," Josh replied, clamping a hand down on his friend's shoulder, "That bastard won't even know what hit him." The two walked off, heading for lunch, cracking jokes and laughing just like old times. They met Mizuki and Willam at the cafeteria, they enjoyed a lunch together.

"So, Willam, Alex, Mizuki, you guys want to go visit Spencer?" Josh asked, "I hear he's in a good enough state to talk!"

"Sorry Josh, but after Alexis, I don't think I could stand seeing another victim of *his*," Mizuki replied.

"I understand," Josh commented.

"Oh shit, Josh! I just realized I'm re-writing an exam in six minutes! I really have to go!" Alex exclaimed, dashing out the door. Willam nodded at Josh, and the two stood up, leaving the building.

"Did you hear the official report for the killings?" Willam asked.

"No, but there's no way they can cover this one up," Josh replied.

"They're calling it 'Suicide by Murder'. Saying that the guys just wanted to kill themselves, but were too chicken shit to do it, so killed some others so that the guards would put them down!" Willam burst.

"What? That's complete shit! Why wouldn't they just kill each other?" Josh asked,

"Exactly! Plus, only like, three percent of the camp believe this suicide bullshit, but only me, you, Spence, Alex and Mizuki have enough balls to do anything about it!" Willam added. The two continued the rant as they walked the rest of the way to the hospital. Back in the cafeteria, Alex entered the building again, where he found Mizuki sitting in the same booth.

"What about that exam?" She asked.

"That was a lie so that I could get some time with you away from Josh," Alex replied, oozing suave. He took a seat across from Mizuki.

"Interesting," She replied, leaning closer across the table.

"Listen, I really, *really* like you, and I know Josh told you that already, but I thought you should hear it from me. If you want to be with Josh, that's cool, he's a good guy. But I need to know. It's hard to be friends with a guy when every five seconds you want to disfigure him to win the girl!" Alex spoke very quickly, a guard was on his rounds, nearing the table. "But what I'm really asking is... Mizuki, will you go out with me? Or, at least, as much as two people can in a place like this?" Alex asked.

"Yes, Alex, I think that you win," Mizuki smiled, leaning closer. Alex leaned in, and the two locked lips, kissing gently. Josh was the farthest thing from Alex's mind in that moment. Suddenly there was a slam. The guard had whacked his rifle down on the table. Alex and Mizuki broke apart, blushing.

"Keep it PG, you two," The guard reprimanded, then continued on his rounds. Alex and Mizuki waited until he was halfway across the room, then leaned forward and kissed again, passionately. They broke apart quickly, not wanting to be seen.

"Listen, Alex. Tonight the blocks are free later than usual. None of the girls in my Block really like each other, so the place should be deserted. Meet me there. Now, you leave. I will follow you in two minutes. See you tonight," Mizuki whispered to Alex. They quickly kissed again, then Alex stood, striding quickly out of the building, blushing and ecstatic. In the hospital, Josh and Willam stood over the sleeping Spencer. He had a large bandage 'round his midsection. There were specks of blood dotting the wrap, it was obviously still seeping.

Spencer began to stir, mumbling to himself. He slowly opened his eyes, Josh and Willam smiled at him. He smiled back, coughing lightly.

"Water," He mumbled. Josh handed him the glass from his bedside table, Spencer chugged the whole thing. He let out a sigh as he replaced the glass.

"How are you feeling, Spencer?" Willam asked.

"Not bad, Willam, not bad at all. It only stabbed about and inch and a half into me, it hit my pelvic bone. I saw the guy who stabbed me... I swear, as soon as I'm out of here..." Spencer mumbled, starting to fall asleep again.

"He got shot when the guards rushed in to... 'heroically save you'. He's dead, Spencer," Josh informed him.

"Good, 'cause I don't want to serve time in solitary for that swine," Spencer laughed, coughing again. Josh slowly pulled back the covers. There was a bloody bandage around Spencer's ankle.

"That's why I'm still here. The bullet passed straight through. Those damned guards... some way to solve a problem," Spencer grunted as Josh pressed gently on the wound. Josh took Willam aside.

"He doesn't know anything that could serve the case. He should be dead, quite frankly, I should be dead," Josh whispered. Willam nodded, "I think that we should spend the rest of the day investigating the murders, before he comes back to finish me off."

"I agree," Willam whispered, "We need to kill this psychopath before he takes you out. I think we should go talk to the other patients in this ward, I'll go tell Alex to come here, you can go investigate the scene of the original crime. Use that brain of yours."

"Okay, I'll stay with Spencer until you and Alex get back here, then I'll head out," Josh whispered back. The two turned back around, smiling at Spencer, who smiled back, suspicious of their conversation, but hid it well. Josh went and sat beside Spencer, who fell asleep quickly. Josh thought of the crimes, and what Ace would have done if he had been stabbed in the attack. Some minutes later Willam and Alex returned. Josh wandered off to the bloodstained wall, and set to work. He examined the list. Several names had been 'elegantly' scratched off with a red felt pen.

The new list was as so: Josh, Spencer, some man named Edward, some guy named Danton, Willam, a man named Cory, and some guy named Alexander, not Alex. Josh scribbled down the names Edward, Danton, Cory, and Alexander as possible suspects. Josh examined the blood, now dry, and a knife that had been dropped on the ground. Josh had no way to analyze fingerprints, but he was sure that it belonged to someone who had already died. Josh, Spencer and Edward were the only three to survive from the top ten, alongside four 'un listed' casualties. None of those who launched the attack survived.

Josh kicked away the snow around the bloody knife and found a severed finger lying on the ground. Shivers ran down his spine, it was a feeling of nausea unfit to his personality, unfit to his training. The whole event disgusted Josh, but for some reason this finger stood out to him. Josh reached down and picked it up, it was limp. Josh bent the finger back, and found interesting dragging marks across the fingernail. Josh looked at his own right forefinger. The same drag marks. The victim played the guitar.

Josh dropped the finger, and had a lead. He only knew of two other people in the camp with guitars, one from A Block and one from B Block. The guy from A Block had had his guitar confiscated two months ago, his finger would have healed. So Josh set off for B Block, hot on the trail. Josh pulled open the heavy B Block door, slipping into the building. It was extremely dark, Josh pulled a lighter out of his pocket and flicked it on. It offered almost no light, Josh flicked it off, saving gas. He carefully scanned each bunk, looking for the instrument.

After about thirty minutes of searching the massive building, he found the guitar resting against the wall next to a bunk. Josh pulled back the covers, looking for any clues. He pulled up the lid of the trunk, usual items. The only contraband this man had was the guitar. Josh checked the pockets of all the clothes, nothing. Josh was about to give up when he had an idea. He pulled the pillow off the bed, and shook out the contents. A piece of paper floated to the ground. Josh picked it up, and began to read.

Congratulations on finding this note, Josh. It appears you are truly a nemesis to be considered an annoyance. You were looking for any sort of proof that this man had been paid off to stab the others. Well, I thought ahead of you, once again. I replaced that note with this one. Just to annoy you. Well, you have come this far, you deserve a small reward. Another clue can be found in The General's desk. But, I will remove it at nightfall tonight. Good Luck.

Josh was infuriated that the freak had yet again been ahead of him. Josh pocketed the note and straightened the man's bed just as he heard the doors slide open.

"His bed is over this way..." Josh heard one of the guards murmur. Josh thought fast, slipping under the bed adjacent to the victim's. Josh saw three pairs of military boots come into view, and the light of a flashlight illuminate the space.

"Are we alone?" One of the guards asked.

"Completely," A guard replied.

"We need to quickly eradicate any evidence of the murder. We need to keep up the illusion of suicide."

"Why?"

"Because if we don't, he'll stop paying us, and start killing us! The General as well..." Josh was taken aback at this last answer. And then it all then fell into place. The murderer was paying off The General and the guards to keep up the suicide ruse. But Josh was sure he had never shown his face to these men, he was too smart for that. Josh let out his breath, involuntarily. The talking above him stopped. Josh quickly pulled the box of matches Ace had given him on his first day from his pocket, and struck one. He heard one of the guards bending down to look under the bed. His face came into view. Josh threw the match at the man, who drew back in shock. Josh reached for his revolver, then realized that it had been confiscated off Spencer.

Josh scrambled out from under the bunk. He pulled his shirt up over his face to conceal his identity, then pushed through the guards, running for the exit of the Block. He jumped to the right just as the bullet whizzed past, smashing into the wall. Josh slipped out the still open door, pulling his shirt down and blending into a crowd of passing students. He wiped the sweat from his brow, catching his breath. If he had been seen, he would have been taken to solitary for sure, just to keep him quiet. But this was an amazing revolution. The murderer was paying off the officials. Josh found Alex in their Block, learning a G chord from Willam.

"Did you get anything from the interviews?" Josh asked.

"No, they're suffering from major post traumatic... blocked the whole thing out," Alex answered, looking up from the strings.

"Well I had a major breakthrough. I uncovered one of the assassin's bunks, and found a note left for *me* from the mastermind behind it all. He said that another clue was hidden in *The General's desk*," Josh informed.

"What? We can't get in there!" Alex panicked. Willam looked shocked.

"I also learned that the psychopath is paying off the guards and The General to pull off this ruse of suicides," Josh added.

"Damn!" Willam yelled, kicking the bed.

"I think I might know a way into The General's office after all, actually..." Alex said after a minute, mulling the idea around in his head.

"Really?" Josh asked.

"What time is it? Quickly, someone, what time?" Alex asked suddenly.

"Fifteen forty six," Josh replied, "Why?"

"I have noticed that The General always visits classes three to four. If we can get in and out in that timeframe, we might be able to do this..." Alex theorized. Josh realized that in this situation, he was the student, and Alex the master. He stepped down, allowing his friend to take charge.

"What next, Alex?" Josh asked.

"Willam, can you find me two ski masks and two smoke grenades?" Alex turned and asked. Willam sprinted out of the Block in the direction of the armory. Josh knew that the lock had been recently broken. Willam came back three minutes later, huffing for breath, holding a brown sack.

"Good. Josh, follow me. We will have to be quick," Alex said, tossing Josh a mask and a smoke grenade. They walked up to the administration offices. Alex nodded at Josh. They came to the first two guards at the door and jabbed them in the solar plexus in unison. They crumpled to the ground, gasping for breath. Josh and Alex pushed through the doors, pulling the masks on. They walked down the hall a ways, then took a left. They came to a hallway filled with guards, doors on either side.

"Gas grenades," Alex said to Josh. The two men activated their grenades at the same time, rolling them under the feet of the seven guards. They went off, effectively blinding their enemies. Alex moved to a door on the right, breaking in. Josh noted the name 'Contraband'.

"Why there?" Josh asked. Alex came back with a gym bag full of cash and four knives. "Why those?" He asked.

"All the downed guards. When the smoke clears, they'll think that we broke in to take this cash. The two moved slightly down the hall. The poison smoke cleared, the guards were down. They would awake in three hours. Josh put his hands out and Alex placed his boot in the hands, lifting him up toward the vent in the ceiling. Alex produced a screwdriver from his back pocket, which befuddled Josh, and removed the grate. He gripped the edge and pulled himself up. A hand reached down from the darkness, and pulled Josh up. Alex then replaced the grate and screwed it back in.

They scuttled along the vent, it was extremely narrow. Alex ditched the knives, and took only two pocketfuls of cash before ditching the bag. They crawled for some twenty seconds, Alex guiding them along several twists and turns. Josh could not stop wondering how Alex knew his way around.

"Here," Alex said. Josh checked his watch. Fifteen fifty four. Alex unscrewed the vent and dropped into the room. Josh dropped in after him.

"I'll search the desk while you replace the grate," Josh ordered. Alex set to work. Josh moved to the desk, pulling open the first drawer. Well, tried to. He jiggled the drawer. It was locked.

"Damn!" Josh exclaimed, "Locked!" Alex swore. Josh searched through the papers on the desk, behind the computer monitor, along the edge of the desk... nothing. Josh knew which drawer the note was in. Second to top on the left side. There was a scratch mark about the keyhole, as if someone had picked it. Suddenly there was a scratching at the door. Josh and Alex stared at each other.

"He's not supposed to be back for another five minutes! He's always exact!" Alex mouthed to Josh.

"Why are we here again, sir?" Josh heard an unfamiliar voice from behind the door.

"I was tipped off that somebody was going to be breaking into my office," The General's voice replied. Josh went rigid. The killer... he was testing Josh. Josh knew that the air of mystery was up. Josh ripped the mask from his head and wrapped it around his fist, wound up, and punched through the thin wood of the desk drawer. It slid open. Josh grabbed all the papers in the drawer and shoved them in his pocket.

"Where is that key?" The General's voice asked. Josh had some time, "Ah, there it is!" Josh heard the key slide into the lock. Alex ran, smashing through the window near the desk, falling three stories into the bushes below. Josh stood and ran for the window as the door began to open. As he flew through the window, his ankle caught on some broken glass, shredding the skin. Josh's boot disappeared past the frame as The General burst into the room. He ran to the broken window, looking first below, then grabbing the shredded, bloody cloth that was caught on the windowsill.

"A student..." The General surmounted. He smirked. Down below, Josh held Alex in the bush, against his will.

"The General will look down here for sure!" Josh whispered angrily to Alex. After twenty seconds, Josh took his hand off Alex's mouth and stood up cautiously, testing the weight on his bleeding leg. He limped off with the assistance of Alex, holding one of the masks against the wound, ebbing the bleeding. They struggled through the front door of the Block, Josh collapsed onto his bunk.

"We need to get you to the medical ward," Alex said, examining the wound for the first time.

"No... the glass in that window, it's tinted. The only tinted glass in the camp is in The General's office. When they remove it from my leg... they would trace it back," Josh grunted through waves of pain. Alex knew what was going to happen, but didn't want to accept it. Josh pulled a t-shirt from his trunk, balled it up, and bit down on it. He exposed his leg, and waited. Alex left and came back seconds later with a pair of tweezers. When the cold steel first entered Josh's leg, he bit harder on the shirt, sweat appeared on his brow and his muscles tensed. Alex, not being a professional surgeon, had to dig around inside Josh's leg before he found the first piece of glass.

Alex pulled out the large piece of bloody glass and placed it in the trashcan not too far away. Alex went back in again, the tweezers sinking past Josh's skin, unleashing a squirt of blood at Alex. He held open the wound and peered inside.

"Good news or bad news?" Alex asked. Josh took the t-shirt out of his mouth and quickly panted 'good news', the pain was unbearable.

"Good news is it seems that the bone is still completely intact," Alex smiled. Josh was relieved, "Bad news is that the impact with the ground shattered one large piece of glass into hundreds of tiny fragments. We don't have enough time to remove them all," Alex frowned. Josh took the t shirt out of his mouth, panting and grunting in pain.

"Go to the kitchen. Steal approximately eight ounces of sugar. Come back here as soon as possible, I'll be waiting," Josh ordered.

"Where would you go?" Alex asked. He dashed out of the Block. Josh pressed the t shirt against his leg, attempting to hold back the bleeding. Alex returned sometime later. The Block was deserted. He was holding a small brown package. He placed it on Josh's side table, and opened it. The white powder flowed over the sides of the paper.

"Now, I need you to pack the wound full of sugar," Josh demanded. Alex was shocked.

"What?" He asked.

"Ace was once shot twice in the back in the field. His partner stuffed the bullet holes full of sugar, two weeks later, when they removed the bandages, it was solid flesh," Josh explained through heavy breaths. His sheets were blood stained.

"But... the glass shards will be in your leg permanently, sealed into your muscle!" Alex exclaimed.

"As soon as we get out of the camp, I will have them surgically removed, that's only about five months..." Josh grunted. Alex accepted that it was the only course of action. He took a handful of sugar and shoved it into the hole in Josh's leg. Josh bucked, it stung. Alex packed it down with his thumb, then packed in more sugar. The powder was instantly stained red. Alex was sweating with stress. Josh had replaced the shirt in his mouth. Soon the sugar was packed down to the edge of the wound.

"We don't have any bandages!" Alex suddenly realized.

"There is... a roll of duct tape in my nightstand," Josh grunted.

"Are you joking?" Alex asked.

"It was originally designed for surgical purposes," Josh grunted. Alex reached over and grabbed the tape. Josh ripped the sleeve off his shirt and held it over the wound. Alex placed the duct tape on Josh's wound, wrapping the entire leg, around and around, eight times before cutting the tape and flattening it down. Josh lay there, catching his breath, it still hurt like hell.

"I'll just wear long pants for a while, until I can remove the tape," Josh panted. Alex nodded, checking his watch.

"Dinner. Can you walk?" Alex asked. Josh slowly stood up, testing the weight on his leg.

"Yeah, I think I'm fine," Josh reported, grunting with pain. Josh changed his pants, burying the bloody pants in the bottom of his chest. He limped out of the room, attempting to hide the look of the injury. He and Alex made their way up to the cafeteria, suspicious of everybody who glanced at them. They took a seat at a random bench, Josh put his leg up to hold the bleeding. Alex left to get them both meals. Josh spotted Willam coming into the room and waved to him. Willam took a seat next to Josh, spotted his leg up, but said nothing about it. Alex returned with one meal, looking disappointed.

"They wouldn't let me take two meals," He said, pushing the tray across to Josh. Josh knew he should decline the offer, but he needed the protein to heal. He dove into the split pea soup, heartily enjoying every bite. He then ate the bread, scooping up the remainder of the soup. It was a small dinner, he noticed Alex's mind seemed to be elsewhere.

Alex met Mizuki in her Block later that night. They kissed passionately, hands all over each other. She pulled off Alex's shirt, revealing the scarred muscles beneath. He pulled her tank top off, dropping it to the floor. She pushed him onto her bunk and fell on top of him. Josh watched all of this from the window, hidden in the shadows. Josh was furious that Alex had finally won the game, and he was winning it as Josh watched. Josh dropped from the window, rage building in him. He stormed off to The General's office, determined to get his revenge.

"Hello, Josh!" Spencer called from up ahead on the path. When Josh came to him he shoved him backward, flying into a bush. Josh would not be distracted. He came to The General's door, hammering on it with his clenched fist, knuckles white. The General flung the door open, bags under his eyes, reading glasses on his nose.

"What, Josh?" He demanded in his usual cold tone.

"I would like to report misconduct," Josh said in a very steady voice, unwavering.

"What is this misconduct?" The General asked.

"Sexual activity in Block E, Alex, sir," Josh reported. The General was shocked at this betrayal.

"Thank you for telling me, Josh," The General said. He called two guards into his office. "Head over to E Block and arrest the two inmates you will find there," The General ordered. The guards saluted, turned, and left the room. The General took a seat behind his desk, then motioned for Josh to take a seat across from him. The General noticed his slight limp as he sat.

"Now, lets discuss why you broke into my desk earlier today..." The General began. Josh was taken by surprise, but still kept a complete poker face. The General stared at him for a few seconds, before laughing and leaning back. "Haha, you have passed the test, Josh, you're off the hook..." His serious demeanor returned startlingly "for now," The General threatened. Josh let out a breath. He stood up to leave, "Where are you going?" The General asked, "It is camp policy that an accused may face his accuser!" Josh suddenly realized that this may have been the wrong decision.

Back in E block, Mizuki and Alex lay naked next to each other, faces flushed, breathing heavily. Suddenly the door burst open, five guards stormed into the room. Mizuki was the first to react, she jumped from the bed and ran to the showers, two guards were sent in after her. Two guards came and grabbed each of Alex's arms. The third guard ordered him to put pants on, then the two guards dragged him out of the Block, the third followed. Alex was carried all the way to The General's office, where he stood shirtless, he did not see Josh.

"What am I being accused of?" Alex asked like an idiot.

"Sexual activity. This is a very serious offense here at the camp," The General stated, straight faced.

"And who is accusing me?" Alex asked.

"That would be me," Josh said, standing and turning to face Alex. There was a moment of silence between the two of them, then Alex launched at Josh, aiming for his neck.

"I'll fucking kill you you son of a bitch!" Alex yelled. The guards caught him just in time, forcing him to his knees on the ground.

"Sir," Alex raged at The General, "I would like to report a crime." Josh suddenly realized the massive tactical error that had occurred.

"Go on..." The General prompted, leaning forward in interest.

"Inmate Joshua Stone has committed the following heinous crimes: Attempted premeditated murder, contraband, skipping classes, aiding and abetting cheating on a final exam, and worst of all, conspiracy and fraud through the investigation of these so called murders," Alex replied, glaring at Josh the entire time.

"In my defense," Josh retorted, "Alex has assisted me in all of these crimes, including attempted murder." The room fell silent, The General staring intently at the two men.

"I thought you two were friends," The General finally said.

"I thought we were too," Josh spat at Alex. The General nodded at the guards, and they grabbed Josh and Alex. Josh thought of the note from the killer in his bloody pant pocket, buried at the bottom of his trunk. The crucial piece of evidence that would forever remain unread.

"Joshua stone and Alex Whittemore, you have both been sentenced to two months of solitary confinement, effective immediately."

CHAPTER TEN

Josh and Alex were loaded into a truck before it departed through the main gate of the camp, traveling along the road for some twenty miles. They were sitting on opposite sides of the spacious back bed, guards on either side of them. They had been stripped down to underwear, and had no way of getting out. The door to the carriage locked on the outside. Suddenly the truck pulled to a stop, in a billow of dust. A small slit opened in the heavy door, two eyes peered in, then the slit slid closed again. For a brief moment Josh had caught a glimpse of the moon. It was beautifully white, flawlessly full. There was muffled talking outside, then the sounds of heavy machinery moving. The first set of gates. The truck stopped two more times, three gates total.

      Josh quickly ran the odds, taking into consideration number of guards, and the distance between the gates. Forgetting about getting out of the main building, it was a one in three thousand six hundred and twenty four point four percent chance of escape. But then what? Josh would be free, able to create his own life instead of the path that had been set for him. He would move to some small island off the coast of Italy, buy a house with the money he still had in his bunk, which would probably be removed while he was gone, and become... a fisherman. A nice quiet life as a fisherman. Away from all the death and blood.

It was then that Josh realized that he lived for the violence, he was bored without it. He had become accustomed to the sound of a gunshot, the terror of your life in your hands, he thrived on it. It was then that Josh realized he could never have a normal life, he would die a killer.

Stop thinking Josh thought to himself, *you have two months of nothing but thinking. Just clear your mind.* Suddenly the heavy door of the truck slid open. Josh was escorted out first, followed closely by Alex. They blinked in the harsh light, the truck had been extremely dark. Josh was taken into a small white room. It was two feet by two feet, a single lightbulb above, and pearly blank walls. Josh would surely go insane within two days. He prayed that it wasn't his cell. It wasn't. A small slot opened in one of the walls and a set of clothing was pushed through. Josh pulled on the thick black shirt and black pants. Ten seconds later a wall of the room slid open, and Josh stepped out.

He was in a long hallway, a door stationed every four feet along both sides of the hall. Josh thought of Alcatraz, the two prisons shared startling similarities. The two guards led him barefoot far down the hall, forced him to turn left, a door was waiting ajar. The two guards shoved him in and slammed the door behind him. It was dim, Josh could barely see a foot ahead of him. He felt along the edge of the wall. In his head he could see the cell, it was roughly three feet by six feet, a single bed in the back right corner, a toilet in the back left corner. There was a gracious open space in the center of the room. The walls were solid, there wasn't even a seam at the door. There was a grate for a roof, about seven feet above Josh's head. Seven more feet above the grate was the solid concrete ceiling.

There was a walkway that ran along the top of each cell that guards patrolled, being able to look down into your room. Josh assumed that the chamber would get more light in the day, he was wrong. He had no way of keeping time, but when he woke he would scratch a mark on the wall with a piece of rubble he had found on the ground. *Two months is approximately sixty days*, assuming he would sleep more than usual he rounded that down to approximately fifty three marks. Josh knew he could do it. He would suffer massive physical damage in here, they got quarter rations, leftovers from camp, all the nutritional ingredients was gone. He would begin an intense workout routine to keep in shape, and starve himself for the first three days, therefore tricking himself into thinking he was eating more later.

    Josh was exhausted from the tense situation in The General's office. He collapsed onto the bed, there was no pillow. With no airflow through the room, it was blisteringly hot. Josh stripped to his underwear, bunching the clothes up under his head as a pillow. Several seconds later a guard shone a flashlight on him from above, yelling at him to clothe himself again. Josh pulled the clothes back on, boiling in his skin. The thing that really got him was the silence. Being alone was fine, it would give him time to think about life. But the silence was stifling, nobody coughed, nobody sneezed, it was enough to make a man crazy. He guessed that was the point. Josh had never heard such silence... completely devoid of all noise... not even the buzz of a lightbulb two rooms away. Silent. The kind of silence that peers into your soul and mocks your deepest fears.

    Josh had heard a scrape to his left, startling in the blackness of the soundscape. There was somebody in the cell beside him, and the door to his right had slid closed, Alex was there. Josh lay on his back with his eyes closed, and he escaped the cell. He was flying over the woods, back to camp, where Spencer was laying asleep in the medical ward, Willam was laying awake, curious about the two empty bunks some six rows down from him.

    "Josh, where are you?" He asked. Josh woke up suddenly, breathing heavily. The dream had been incredibly realistic, probably boosted by the silence and absolute black. Josh wondered if it was more than a dream, if his friends really had discovered his absence yet. Josh wasn't tired anymore, he must have been asleep for a while, although it only seemed like seconds. There was a tray at the foot of his bed, it had been placed there while he slept. Upon this tray Josh found a misshapen hard boiled egg, a small piece of buttered toast, and a cup of cold coffee. Josh guessed the time was around nine thirty, judging by the length of the drive and the time breakfast was served at camp.

    Josh realized a flaw in his starvation plan. The egg would go bad, and begin to smell. Josh quickly made his way over to the toilet and tossed the food, making sure a guard was not above. Josh set to pacing. He crossed the cell in three paces before he would spin and walk back. Josh walked for hours. A tray of lunch foods was slid under the door, he ignored it. His stomach ached, he wanted to eat badly, but the sounds that his stomach generated kept him company, and he would never kill it. He paced until his legs began to ache and the wound on his leg burned like it was fresh, he kept pacing. The more exhausted he was, the quicker he would fall asleep, the faster he would get out of this hell. And that was truly the breaking point. The fact that one would hurt oneself just to be entertained, just to have something to think about.

    Josh had to go through the horrible event of having to use the toilet on his second day. It didn't have a lid, he had to squat above the hole. The toilet didn't flush, that would generate too much noise. Instead it burrowed downward an impossibly far distance to moving water below. He continued pacing. Dinner was pushed under the door, Josh continued pacing. At the end of the day he collapsed onto his bed, legs throbbing, exhausted.

    As he drifted off he left his cell again, he saw Spencer and Willam being informed of Josh's detainment, and their looks of worry. Josh realized that as long as he could leave his cell at night, see his friends, hear them talking, he just might get out of there sane. Josh fell asleep sometime later, smiling. He was awoken violently, two guards were holding him down against the bed, he was completely restrained. Josh struggled slightly, but gave up when the syringe entered his flesh. The guards left as quickly as they had come. The experience never occurred again. Josh had trouble falling asleep, but eventually managed to escape his cell once again. He theorized of misconduct to have interaction with the guards, some form of human contact. But somewhere deep in his mind, he knew that one outburst, and something doubly awful as the petrifying silence would occur. His mind, for a brief moment, flashed on a black door labeled 101, and shuddered. Something he had read...

    A few days later, Josh's eyes had adjusted to the extreme dark, and he took the time to calculate the date. He realized that he was spending his birthday, that day, in solitary. They had never truly celebrated birthdays at the orphanage, but Josh still felt sad about being *as alone as possible* on the date of his coming to existence. He took the bread from his dinner and placed it on a space of floor he had not trodden on, it was covered in dust. He drew a cake design around the bread, complete with eighteen candles. Josh thought of Mason, his old friend, his closest ally. He wondered if Mason had ever been sent to solitary. Josh ate the bread, he could almost taste the chocolate and cherry... He fell asleep quickly that night, feeling more mature somehow.

    Josh woke up, marked his wall, and set to pacing. Halfway through the day he dropped to the floor and began doing pushups and sit-ups, switching between pacing and this throughout the day. He eat the meager rations he was given. He suspected that the guards were stealing his food, it seemed too meager, even for leftovers. Josh knew he needed to stop thinking like that, paranoia would only speed insanity. He continued pacing. He collapsed once again on his bed at the end of the day, exhausted once again. The glass shards stuck in his leg burned, reminding him he was still human. This schedule continued until Josh had managed to make it to twenty five marks. *Halfway there.* Josh celebrated silently, letting himself eat everything when it was given to him, instead of in small portions throughout the day. Josh continued working out, it would be too monotonous to give up on it. He was halfway through, and he had managed to keep up his mental and physical health.

On that day, Josh heard the first noise he had heard other than his own intestines grumbling. Alex screamed out from the cell to Josh's right, cursing the guards, screaming for water. The sudden, startlingly loud noise hit him like a boulder, he fell to his knees clutching his ears. Josh heard Alex's door open, a whack, then he was silent. Josh worried for his friend's mental state. He didn't know if he would even connect with the man that emerged from that cell, if a man emerged at all. Two days later, Josh found a small note hidden under his toast. Josh unfolded it silently, laying under his bed, and read it in the weak light.

Josh, you are halfway through. I hope you still have your faculties about you, I know that two weeks did quite the number on me. Things have turned to shit since you left, Josh. They are cracking down, taking all contraband, increasing curfew, and allowing harsher punishments. Twelve people have been sent to solitary so far. *Spencer is out of the hospital, his leg got infected, he's on crutches now. They haven't looked into the murders at all, that poor man Danton was lit on fire, we could hear him screaming a mile away. Some kid named Cory has moved into top place on the leader board, so I'm keeping an eye on him. Anyway, I managed to hide your guitar from the guards, I know it's special to you. I found your revolver when I was in a holding cell a week ago, brought it back with me. Hope you manage another month, you're almost there!*
    Willam H. Blackburn II

Josh quickly threw the paper down the toilet. If it was found, Willam would be punished more harshly than Josh would. Josh had no idea how much it had cost Willam to get the note to him, but he would pay him back the second he got out of solitary. Josh continued pacing, hopes rising. Pacing, pacing, pacing. Sleep was as irrelevant as happiness. He felt exhausted all the time, but continued pacing, he was nothing without it. One two three, turn. One two three, turn. One two three, turn. One two three, Turn. He had become a finely tuned machine, no longer a human but a robot doing the bidding of his captors, accepting his dreary lot in life. His entire humanity had deteriorated to a pendulum, a metronome as one might find in a school band room. Finally Josh awoke one day to mark the fifty third mark on his wall. Halfway through that day, Josh's door slid open. The light from the hall blinded him, searing his retinas, causing him to fall to his knees, clutching at his eyes. Sound erupted into his ears, invading his mind, tearing his insides out, wrenching his very soul.

Two guards came forward and clasped either of Josh's arms, dragging him out of the cell, into the light. Josh's eyes slowly adjusted to the light. He saw the two shadowy shapes of the guards standing on either side of him, and three shadowy figures slightly further down the hall. Josh slowly began to make out details. The two guards standing next to him were the same two that had put him in the cell. *How poetic.* Alex was laying on the ground down the hall, he looked horrible. His eyes were sunken, his face thinned, he looked like a walking skeleton. Alex turned his head to look at Josh. In his eyes he saw the definition of insanity; how far a man could go.

Josh began to move toward him, Alex made his way to his feet. Josh and Alex came together in a brotherly embrace.

"Josh, I'm sorry I put you in that hell," Alex cried through a dusty, unused throat.

"No, Alex, it was me, I'm sorry that I ratted you out," Josh replied, his hoarse voice surprised him. Alex collapsed to the ground suddenly. The two guards helped him up.

"What's going to happen to him?" Josh asked.

"He's pretty bad, he'll be taken to an intensive care ward for about a month, he'll be put on a pure vitamin and protein diet, later we'll put him on an intensive workout routine, then some psychological tests to ensure his sanity," One of the guards replied. Josh had a feeling this was standard procedure.

"Why the psyche test?" Josh asked. One of the guards pointed to Alex's cell. Josh quickly looked inside. Alex had scratched Josh's name all over the walls, circled, and x'd out. There were drawings of murders, random numerical puzzles, and the most confusing to Josh, Williams's name against the back wall. The rest of that wall was clear. There were even scratches on the floor. One of the guards took Josh's arm. One word came to Josh's mind. *Hate.*

"Ready to head back to camp?" The guard asked. Josh couldn't take his eyes off Alex's cell.

"I... I think so..." Josh stuttered, turning from the insanity. The guard led him away. Josh stepped into the same small white room he had been in when he entered the cell, two months ago. The memory was startlingly vivid. A tray was sticking out of the wall. Josh figured it out. He removed his black prisoner's clothing and placed it in the tray. His skin was filthy. The tray slid back into the wall, his old clothes were returned to him, and the door opened. The two guards were awaiting him. They escorted him out and onto the bus. Josh fell asleep on the long ride. When the bus pulled to a stop in front of the camp, Josh awoke, and remembered his first day. It seemed like so long ago. The stifling heat had returned to the air, telling Josh he was nearing of the end of his torturous journey.

Josh stepped off the bus, his legs wobbling not from weakness but from exhaustion. He staggered to his bunk, pulling on his casual clothes, and set off for the dining hall. It was time for a proper meal. He pushed through the door and was practically tackled by Spencer in a cumbersome bear hug. Josh staggered backward, nearly smashing to the ground.

"Josh, you're okay!" Spencer exclaimed. Josh smiled weakly, still not sure of his own psyche. He hugged Spencer back. Spencer stepped away, allowing Willam to give Josh a hug.

"I got your note," Josh whispered in his ear, not wanting a guard to overhear them. Josh noticed that Mizuki was not there, possibly in solitary, possibly dead. He would not see her again for a very long time. Josh moved into the room, the inmates stood up clapping. He had survived what befell so many. Josh again pondered if Mason had been subjected to solitary. Would he even recognize his old friend? Josh took a seat in the back left corner of the room, Spencer brought him a large sandwich and a bowl of soup. Josh devoured it heartily. He drained some seven cups of coffee.

Josh stepped into his Block, testing his weight. He came to his bunk and lay on the bed. It was much more comfortable than the one in solitary. Willam entered the bathrooms and came back with Josh's guitar, handing it to him tentatively. Josh took it and hid it under his sheets. He stood up and made his way to the bathroom, he carefully looked in the mirror.

He was sporting a four inch neck beard, sunken eyes, chapped lips, and a cracked tooth. Josh did not remember cracking the tooth. He ran back to his bunk, grabbed his razor, and shaved his face. With each hair that fell to the floor, Josh felt his freedom returning. Once he was clean shaven, he belonged to the camp once again. He took a long shower, washing away the memories. He spent the rest of the day with his friends, basking in the vices of the 'free world'. Josh didn't realize it, but he had been completely corrupted. He thought of being at the camp as freedom now.

The next two weeks were hectic for Josh. He had to take every quiz and test that had occurred while he was in solitary. Josh came out without major damage to his grade, he had slipped by mostly on logic. But the final exam was coming fast. It wasn't like the others. It wasn't a written test or a Block war, it was a *'survival intensive'*. Five men, dropped in the woods, with nothing but their clothes, left there for a week. Usually only three or four men returned. But death was normal at the camp now. Each and every inmate had accepted the possibility of fate striking them at any moment.

Alex returned from the medical ward soon after Josh finished his tests. He seemed completely recovered, physically strong and mentally stable. But Josh could tell that something was wrong behind his eyes, like he had stared into the void, and didn't quite come back.

"Hey Alex," Josh said one day while they were sitting on the dock, skipping rocks.

"Yeah?" He asked.

"Those things on your cell walls..." Josh began. He had seen the scratches over and over again, playing like a broken tape through his mind.

"Josh, they've wiped the past two months from my mind. I only remember my first week in solitary. But it was... *awful*. I have no idea how you got through it sane," Alex tremored, standing up.

"Hello Josh, Alex," The General said, approaching the two men. They just glared at him, resenting him for sending them to that place. They had begun to revolt against the structure of the camp, and had skipped the camp meeting earlier that day. "I noticed you weren't at the meeting. I thought you should know that the groups for the final exam has been posted, its done in groups of five by grade. You two, Willam, Spencer, and Cory are together at the top of the list, so you all will be heading out into the woods together," The

General informed them. The two looked at each other and had a small wordless conversation.

Josh was top of the class, even after solitary, and this Cory character was one below him. There had been next to no murders while Josh was in solitary... and suddenly Josh knew who the killer was. And he was about to spend a week alone in the woods with him. Josh gulped, beginning to sweat. The General turned to leave, then whipped around to add one more point.

"And if either of you misbehave again, so help me God, you will be expelled from this program. The best job you will get at the I.E.M.F. would be a janitor. That means no investigation into these so called 'murders'. You hear me?" The General asked.

"Yes, Sir!" Josh and Alex answered in unison. The General left. Two hidden guards following him.

"We could always pay someone off to kill this Cory before we head out," Alex suggested.

"No, all my money, and yours, was confiscated while we were in solitary. It would cost more than anybody else at camp has... there's no way. He won't kill me until we head out though, the situation is too good," Josh replied. The two made their way back to their Block, Josh to play guitar and Alex to fiddle with Josh's revolver. The rest of the day passed quickly, and without event. There was one week remaining before they departed for the forest.

CHAPTER ELEVEN

"How do you think he sleeps at night?" Josh asked his friends. They were sitting on a park bench, eyeing Cory cautiously.

"Well, at least we're all together..." Willam started, trailing off into oblivion.

"That is a point," Spencer added, "We could always overpower him in the bush if he makes a move."

"Exactly!" Willam exclaimed. Alex was silent, watching the basketball bounce up and down some twenty feet away. Alex's head was spinning. He had no idea what had happened in that cell, but he had a horrible feeling that he had solved the murders, and that it wasn't Cory. He didn't say any of this to his friends, it could quite possibly turn them on each other.

"That brings up another point," Josh said suddenly. The others turned to look at him. "Alex and I don't have any more money. I know we can't pay off the guards to help you cheat on this, they take it too seriously. But I was thinking, could we pool our money and get our hands on a remote carabiner?" Josh asked.

"A what?" Spencer asked.

"It's like a basic carabiner, but at the push of a button it releases. We could attach a sack of out supplies to the bottom of the helicopter, hide the remote inside the chopper, and release the sack when we land," Josh explained.

"That won't work..." Willam explained.

"Why not?" Spencer asked. Alex was silent.

"One group already came back from the exam. They were hidden from us, they had suffered too much. Horrible wounds and the like, I heard from one of them that you parachute in, for that exact reason..." Willam explained.

"Damn it!" Josh cursed, plan thwarted. The four men watched Cory play basketball, wondering how a psychopath could act so normally. *Six days.*

Josh couldn't sleep. He tossed and turned in his bed. Images of the bodies and the evidence flashed through his mind. He heard the scream played over and over again, felt Alexis's blood on his hands. He was trying to connect it all, trying to match the actions to the face, but something didn't add up. Josh had seen something that threw the theory off... *but what was it?* He searched his memory, seeing all the events that had occurred... Ten minutes of memory was missing... *what was it?* Josh asked himself.

He gave up on sleep, standing from his bunk and silently padding across the Block. He came to the door and climbed out the window as he had before. The door guards were absent this night. Josh wandered around the yard, stopping only once. He came to a street lamp and saw a figure standing under it. Josh slowly moved toward him, cautious. He recognized it as Cory. He was just standing there, staring up at the light, not moving. This deeply troubled Josh, it just seemed so... unnatural. *Five days.*

Josh and Alex were at the firing range, enjoying their last days with the weapons. Josh had unlocked the secrets of sniping, and was battling Alex to pick off set targets before him. Josh always lost, but it was still fun. Josh scoped the last target, a dummy sniper laying in the grass a distance away.

Josh pulled the trigger, just as blood exploded from the dummy.

"Ha! I win!" Alex exclaimed, fist pumping. Josh took his eye from the scope, feeling defeated.

"Yeah, *again!* Damn, how are you so good at this?" Josh asked.

"Chin up Josh, you're still slightly better than your average guy..." Alex chuckled back. Josh heard a snort of laughter from behind him. Josh turned to see Cory standing slightly behind them, staring down ominously. A chill ran along Josh's spine. There was a blank look in his eyes, and his jaw was slack. Josh and Alex went back to sniping, not wanting to let on an air of suspicion. *Four days.*

"Josh, we need to do something about Cory..." Spencer started, the four men sat around a small campfire in the yard. It was dark. The laws of the camp had become far more lenient as the year drew to an end.

"I agree. I've seen him staring at me, acting really weird," Willam added. Josh stood, to emphasize his point.

"We must wait until we get to the forest. There, we can make it look as if he choked to death, or just wandered off and died. Then, we will be off the hook. If we take care of him now, it may cost us our passing grade," Josh announced in a loud, unwavering voice. Josh sat back down.

"I agree with Josh. Together we can withstand him, battle the elements, and get out of this camp respectively, but we must wait. He can't kill any of us if at least two are awake at all times," Alex added. The other two men nodded. Suddenly Cory slipped from the shadows, taking a seat between Josh and Alex. Josh worried that he had heard the entire conversation. The fire gleamed wildly in his eyes.

"Well, boys, we are going out in the woods together for a week. We need to talk strategy, and get to know each other. It'll be better if we're friends," Cory laughed. The other four chuckled, nervously.

"Well, I'm..." Josh started.

"Josh, Alex, Willam, Spencer," Cory stated, pointing at each one respectively, "You guys are kind of like celebrities around the camp. I was worried that the camp was split into grades for the campout, but then I realized it was with you guys... Now I'm not worried about getting stabbed in my sleep, or hung, or burned... thats for sure," Cory laughed. The others chuckled, edging away slightly.

"Well, nice meeting you Cory," Willam started, extending his hand to the man, who shook it vigorously.

"Oh, look at the time, I've got to go," Cory said, standing and leaving the group. Josh watched him go, cautious of the man.

"Ruse to cover his tracks?" Alex asked.

"Definitely," Josh confirmed. *Three days.*

Josh, Alex, Spencer, and Willam lounged around Josh's bunk, Josh was strumming his guitar. More groups had returned from the forest, and all were taken directly to the hospital. Josh had never talked to anybody who had returned. They were sworn to secrecy on the subject. Josh's group would ship out third to last.

"Hey, Josh," Willam asked suddenly.

"Yeah?" Josh responded.

"If one of us does get killed, what will happen to the dynamic of the group? Will we completely disperse? I mean, I don't really see Alex being here if you get killed..." Willam asked.

"The way I see it..." Josh began, setting the guitar down, "You and Spencer are like, best friends. All those little adventures you two go off on when me and Alex are busy or caught up in some heavy handed, over dramatic stuff are hilarious. If Alex or I get killed, I see you two sticking together forever. And if one of you get killed... I don't know, I think that the other would be an emotional wreck. I know that Spencer would remain friends with me, but between you two and Alex, there really isn't that much interaction," Josh explained.

"Hm, I never realized that," Alex replied.

"Interesting..." Willam trailed off. The four men sat there, disheartened by the heavy talk. Cory suddenly appeared out of nowhere, just walking past the bed, staring at the four men. Josh glared back, not intentionally. He felt nothing but hatred for anybody that would dare break apart their tightly knit group. *Two days.*

"Man, it has been a long, hard road, but looking back, it doesn't really seem like a year, does it?" Alex asked, dribbling the basketball as Spencer waved his arms around in front of him, blocking. Alex twisted on his left foot and bounced the ball under Spencer's arm, right into Josh's hands. Josh dribbled the ball forward, spun around Willam, jumped, and slammed the ball, hanging on the net a second before dropping back to the ground.

"Well, that's because you've had two months of it wiped from your mind! That solitary was one of the longest experiences of my life... It feels like it's been five years!" Josh exclaimed, wiping the sweat from his brow. Willam bounced the ball a few times, bounced it to Josh, who bounced it back. Willam dribbled forward, tossing to his left just as Josh came in front of him, Spencer caught it. Spencer came forward and shot, Alex smashed the ball out of the air and dribbled it back down the court. Willam was coming up on him, Alex threw the ball from far back, Josh ran up and nicked it with the tip of his finger, the ball redirected into the net.

"A three!" Josh exclaimed.

"Technically, you tapped the ball while your hand was over the three line..." Spencer argued.

"But my feet were on the three line!" Josh exclaimed. After a short argument Josh's team gained two points.

"But... excluding solitary... it does seem kind of short, doesn't it?" Willam asked. Willam took off down the court, dribbling fast. Alex lunged at him, Willam caught the ball for a second then returned to dribbling, still moving.

"Foul!" Alex called, pointing at Willam. Willam passed the ball back to Alex, who took two steps before tossing the ball at Josh, who shot a J, bouncing the ball off the backboard at a ten degree angle and catching the edge of the net.

"You guys are getting dominated!" Josh exclaimed, laughing.

"Now that you say it, it has gone by rather quickly..." Spencer finally answered. The four men took a seat, enjoying some water.

"It's been pretty harsh, too..." Josh added.

"The poker beating..." Alex murmured.

"Yes! The poker beating!" Josh laughed. He had completely forgotten about the experience. The men spent the rest of the day recalling their experiences at the camp, laughing and crying together, reliving the entire experience in intense detail. Cory watched and listened from a short distance away. *One day.*

Josh woke early that day, he only had one more night in that bed. He would be moved to *'specialty housing'* after the forest event. Those that passed the experience, in other words, *survived,* and had a grade of ninety and above, were moved to a luxurious building, with feather beds and television. Josh looked forward to the experience. Once these few, very few, men were in the building, a quarter of them would be chosen to join the agency. Then five of those remaining men would be chosen to become agents. Ah, yes, the ultimate goal. Becoming an agent of the the International Extreme Missions Force. It was the goal that united the men and women in the camp. There would be a luxurious award ceremony on the last day, just before they were taken back to their respective places of origin.

Alex was awake as well. The two retrieved a mug of steaming coffee, then made their way down to the dock, sitting and watching the sun rise over the water.

"Josh, what is the first thing you will do when you return home?" Alex asked.

"I think the first thing I will do is have a good shower. Have you noticed that the water here varies in temperature wildly every two seconds?" Josh asked.

"Yeah," Alex replied, "how could I not?".

"Then I'm gonna buy myself a fine suit, and sport it around the place. And I'll eat a good, heaping burger from this little place Ace used to bring me takeout from," Josh added.

"Sounds nice... I don't know where I'll be going back too... I came straight from the prison, and if I pass, I won't be going back..." Alex trailed off. The two men avoided the fact that they might not be going back at all.

CHAPTER TWELVE

Josh, Alex, Cory, Spencer, and Willam were woken at the crack of dawn. Josh pulled on his fatigues and looked longingly at the jacket hung next to his bunk. They were led far from the Blocks by armed, masked guards. They were forced to change into their uncomfortable combat uniforms, frisked, then moved farther from the complex. Josh looked at his three friends. They had all matured and hardened so much since the beginning of camp. Alex had become far more mature, Spencer had learned to keep quiet, and Willam... Willam learned to be more human.

Josh and his group crested a hill and laid eyes on an amazing sight. A small, black helicopter was sitting on the pad at the base of the hill, blades slowly spinning, a large white I.E.M.F. T-4 painted on the side. Josh, Alex, Spencer, Willam, and Cory were brought down to the machine. The large bay door slid open, revealing two guards and The General.

"Welcome to the beginning of the end, boys," The General yelled to them. The blades increased in speed but not volume. The two guards in the chopper reached down, first pulling Alex and Spencer, then Josh and Cory, and finally Willam into the vehicle. It was startlingly cavernous on the inside. The door was slid shut, the four guards on the ground saluting goodbye. The General and the two guards took seats at the front of the helicopter, facing back. The boys took their seats in two rows at the back of the chopper, facing the General. They felt the ground drop from under them as they begin to lift into the air, which was disillusioning because the blades generated no noise, just the faint hum of the motor. It had to be the latest technology in stealth craft.

"It's quiet so we can observe you all during the test... without alerting you..." One of the guards answered Josh's silent question. The five inmates looked at each other, wondering what was to come.

"As of now, I can tell you nothing more that may assist you in your survival," The General announced, "You have all learned how to parachute in your training, and if you have forgotten, have a nice fall..." Spencer looked nervous at this. "There is nothing around you for miles, so don't spend your time like idiots searching for some hunting cabin, you will starve to death or be eaten first. I do suggest that you elect a leader, before taking any action on the ground. As you'll notice, there are no windows in this chopper, and we have changed direction twelve times already this flight, so don't try to find your way back to camp. Work as a team. For every member of your group that dies, you lose five percent of your total mark. Your parachutes are under your seats. Feel free to use these however you choose. Any questions?"

"Is there fresh water?" Spencer asked.
"I can't answer that..." The General replied.
"Is there any game in the area?" Cory asked.
"I can't answer that..." The General replied.
"What is your favorite color?" Alex asked.
"Puce," The General replied.
"What's your real name?" Josh asked. The General hesitated a second.

"We are nearing the drop zone," The General said suddenly. The men pulled on the backpacks. The door was slid open. Willam approached first, the wind ripping at his clothes, the look of determination on his face was fierce. The helicopter slowed to a hover.

"You will have no communication with the outside world once you jump..." The General yelled. Willam nodded, springing from the chopper without hesitation. He dropped like a stone. Cory approached the orange square at the door. A guard checked his backpack, then gave him the okay. After a few seconds of hesitation, he jumped. Alex approached next. He didn't wait for the okay. He ran from the other side of the chopper, diving out the door, shouting with joy as he plummeted to earth. Josh smiled at this.

Spencer stood and made his way to the door. On his way by, he whispered to Josh *help me...* Josh knew exactly what he meant. He had forgotten how to parachute. Spencer stood in the doorway, the wind terrifying him, he grabbed either side of the door hole, near vomiting. Josh had a plan. Spencer waited a full thirty seconds, then was kicked from the doorway by a guard. He plummeted to the earth. Josh watched him spread out his body to fall as slowly as possible. Josh looked out the doorway. They were quite a good distance up, he could still see Alex in the air, he had time to execute his plan. He made his way to the door, tightening the strap of the backpack. Suddenly he was caught on the shoulder. It was The General. This hold up could cost Spencer his life. The General leaned forward and whispered into Josh's ear.

"My brother forced me to tell you to head up the hill first thing. Also, you deserve to know, my real name... it's Bruce. Nothing special..." The General gave Josh a good shove on the shoulder, and he fell from the chopper. Josh turned back to see the door slide closed. The General's laughing face was the last thing he saw. The chopper sped off. It was done. Josh refocused himself. He turned to see Spencer a few meters below him. Josh went as straight as a pencil, closing the distance to Spencer.

Josh collided with him mid air, grabbing him by the arm to slow himself. Josh had never skydived before, outside of the camp simulations, but the wind against his body and the intense forces just felt natural.

"Jo-...-an't... -en....-oot!" Spencer yelled, words whisked away by the wind. Josh turned his back to the ground, spun Spencer in the air, and clipped himself to Spencer. He pulled hard on Spencer's ripline, and the parachute erupted from the backpack. It slowed them slightly, but they were falling too fast, the chute ripped from it's chords, flying into the air. The bang as it broke from the cable was deafening. Josh spun, Spencer facing down, hoping that the failed chute had slowed them enough. The others watched this all take place from below. Josh eyed the ground. They were nearly below the lowest possible shoot release elevation... and at these speeds...

Josh focused. He pulled his chord as hard as he could, and the backpack split open. The parachute burst from it's holster, and fanned out into the air. The tug as it caught the wind nearly ripped Josh's arms from their sockets. He tensed his muscles, waiting for the impact...and they slowed. They drifted calmly down through the air, speed decreasing steadily. But it wasn't enough.

They hit the ground hard, smashing down into the clearing. Josh unclipped Spencer seconds before the impact, pushing him out to the left. Spencer hit a fallen log, doubling over, losing his breath. Josh slammed onto the flat ground, cracking a rib and breaking his nose. His leg burned. Alex rushed over and helped him up, worried. Josh coughed some blood, onto Alex's uniform. The blood from Josh's nose streamed into his mouth, he spat it out.

"Are you okay man?" Alex asked. There was a faint ringing in Josh's ears. *A warm welcome.*

"Yeah... how's Spencer?"Josh asked.

"He looks fine..." Willam yelled from across the clearing. Spencer stood slowly. Josh took a head count...

"Where's Cory?" Josh yelled. They heard moaning from under a fallen chute. The four men rushed over to it and pulled it aside. Cory sat there in a pool of blood, a sliver of bone sticking out from his shin at a very bad angle. He was sobbing, his foot was twisted sideways.

"Bloody hell!" Alex yelled. Josh swooped down to Cory's side, examining the wound.

"Bloody indeed... Compound fracture, broke on impact..." Josh proposed. He looked up at Willam. "Go find two thick pieces of wood, as straight as you can get them, and fast. Spencer, if you're okay, find something sharp, maybe a piece of metal off the backpacks...and cut about six feet of parachute cord from my chute. And... Alex, help me move this rock and set Cory up in the shock position," Josh ordered. The men stood around for a bit. "*Now!*" Josh yelled. They spurred into action. Josh and Alex lifted the rock, causing Cory to scream. His foot was shattered as well.

They lay Cory down and raised his wounded leg onto a nearby rock. Josh put a hand on Cory's forehead, trying to calm him. He told Alex to go about his work, then turned his attention to the wound. He examined his hands, they were relatively clean. He told Alex to shove a stick in Cory's mouth, and once that was done, he dove his hands into the man's leg.

Josh maneuvered the exposed bone around until it came to a relatively proper position, then held it there. Cory screamed in pain, but managed not to buck, not wanting to do himself further damage. Josh was proud of thim, even if he was a psychopathic murderer. He saw the ghosts of the men he had killed in his eyes, heard Alexis in his screams. Josh pushed a little more on the bone, Cory screamed. *Payback.*

Willam and Spencer returned. Josh snapped one of the planks a bit shorter, positioned them on either side of Cory's leg, and began to wrap them tightly with the rope. It was so tight, they cut into the clean flesh. Josh affixed the smaller wood to the end of Cory's foot and tied it into the splint. By the time he was done, the entire leg was wrapped in rope, blood stained but secure. Cory went to stand.

"No, no, you mustn't stand. We will move you around, and make do on our own..." Josh stopped him. Cory frowned, not wanting to be disgraced in front of the heroes of the camp. The three other standing men assembled around Josh, awaiting orders.

"Spencer, gather up the backpacks, chutes and rope, leave one chute out. Try to fit the others in their respective backpacks. Willam, scout ahead up that hill there, await us atop the crest. Alex, help me fold this chute and slide it under Cory, we're taking him up after Willam. Let's go," Josh ordered. The men went to their assignments. Josh and Alex folded the chute and managed to get Cory top side. They lifted it carefully, and slowly took him up the hill after Willam. Spencer followed soon behind, lugging the five backpacks with him. Willam was ecstatic atop the hill, pointing at something far below. The men hurried to see what he was so excited about. When the reached the top, Josh almost dropped Cory, his breath was taken.

They were looking down at a large, sun bathed clearing next to a fast paced, wide river. There was a small sand bank surrounded by rocks. There were many tall, large trees around the clearing, that offered lots of shade. There were several berry bushes near the edge of the clearing. Spencer soon joined them, as shocked as Josh.

"It's...perfect!" He exclaimed. Josh pointed to the clearing and nodded, the two men ran down like school children, followed closely by Alex and Josh, carrying Cory. They lay Cory down at the edge of the clearing, under the shade of a tree. Willam and Spencer had begun to strip off their clothing, heading for the river.

"Hey, no!" Josh called, stopping the charade. The two men, like children, looked at him disappointedly, "There is a hell of a lot of work to get done before the sun goes down, and bathing isn't part of it. When your'e done, if there is still light, then maybe you can," Josh ordered. They began to put their clothes back on. Josh stood atop a rock, his three friends surrounded him, awaiting their orders.

"Okay men, we have all gotten to the ground in more or less one piece, and that in itself is quite the feat. But we still must surmount hunger, predators, and the weather. So, we need to set to work. Spencer, you go out and find wood for a fire, pile it in the middle of the clearing. We will need a *lot* of wood, so get it going *fast*. Willam, you will collect twenty rocks about the size of my head next to the wood. Check that, twenty-four. Keep an eye out for any sharp rocks we could use as knives. Once you've finished that, help Spencer with his task. Alex, you will prop Cory up next to those berries over there, then hang one of the chutes about ten feet of the ground in the trees, fully spread, as a roof. Then spread another on the ground, under the one you just hung, pinning each corner with one of the rocks. Cory, find the biggest, ripest berries first, we need a good five pounds of berries. We may need them all day today and tomorrow, depending on how fast we find game. You got it?" Josh asked

The men nodded, then set to work. Josh descended upon the backpacks, stripping them to their most basic parts, most of it would be useless to him. He wrapped the cloth from the packs around five sticks, making facsimile torches. There was nearly no metal on the packs, everything else was useless. He piled them under a tree, behind a large rock to avoid the wind. He took one of the chutes and folded it, twined the ropes together on either end, and found two trees at the edge of the clearing that were a good distance apart. Josh secured the ropes to either tree, making a hammock that hung three feet off the ground. It would be where Cory rested. He walked around and examined the stations. Alex was struggling with the parachutes, Josh helped him to erect the first.

There was now enough wood for a good two hours worth of fire, but not enough. There were seven rocks, and

Cory had collected a pound of berries. Josh was impressed, as he had not eaten a single one. Josh pulled his pants off and spread them out on a rock in the sun, then approached the river. He put a toe in. Even in the searing sun it was freezing. Josh waded out to his waist, about a quarter of the way out into the water. He stood perfectly still, watching the water around him carefully. He stood there, completely motionless, for an hour and a half. He watched the fish swim around his legs, accepting him into their natural habitat.

Josh had figured out the diffraction of the water, and knew exactly where to strike. Finally the opportunity presented itself. Josh dove both hands down, one on either side of his body. His fingers clasped around the scaly, slippery bodies with the strength of a bull. He pulled the fish from the water, struggling, almost slipping from his grip. He smashed one fish's head into the other, the two fish going limp. He threw them back onto the bank, proud of himself. He went still again, waiting another forty-six minutes before clasping his hands around two more fish. Three hours later, he had a pile of seven fish.

"Josh!" Willam called from the bank. Josh looked up, a fish slipping from his grip.

"Yeah?" Josh called back, beginning to wade back to the shore.

"I'm done with the rocks!" He called. Josh came up to the bank and laid out in the sun, drying his cold legs.

"Good... I'm assuming Alex is done as well. I want you two to erect a small wall, blocking off an area in the water about two feet by two feet. When you're done, throw these dead fish in it to preserve them. You need to work quickly, though. Then you two may swim...it'll be hard work," Josh said. Willam saluted him and called Alex over. Josh stood and pulled his pants back on. He made his way over to the wood pile, and was happy to see that it had grown substantially. It covered quite a large area. Spencer came back from the forest, carrying another armful of wood with him, sweat pouring off his brow. He had removed his shirt.

"Hey Spencer," Josh began.

"Yeah?" He asked, dropping the wood on the pile.

"Go help out Willam and Alex... Then go ahead and swim for a bit. This is a really impressive pile you've got here," Josh said. Spencer grinned at him then ran down to Willam. Josh set to work digging out a large hole about a quarter foot deep in the ground, then pushed the large rocks around it, creating a good fire pit. Josh then set to work creating a small teepee of tiny sticks, then average sticks, then the largest of them all. The three layer monstrosity would create a nice big fire. Josh fashioned a fuse leading to the center of the stack with some of the thread from the backpack. He checked the berry bush, there was a good pile of berries started.

"That's a great pile, Cory. We should get two days out of that. You need some rest, you want me to move you to your hammock?" Josh asked. Cory nodded. Josh lifted him and placed him down in his hammock. He fell asleep immediately. Josh went and moved the berries out of the sun, filling one of two still in tact backpacks with them. He moved down to the river and took a long drink of the water. He looked at the sun. It had nearly set. The dead fish were floating in the water, and the other three men were frolicking in the water. As the golden-orange light descended on the clearing, Josh thought that there may actually be hope of getting out of the clearing alive.

Josh picked up two rocks from the shore and moved over to the wood pile, hoping. The odds of one of the two rocks he held containing flint were extremely low, but he could still hope. He crouched over the fuse and slid the rocks against each other. Nothing. Again. Nothing. Josh went back and retrieved two more rocks. Nothing. Another set. Nothing. Josh was about to give up on the eleventh set of rocks when suddenly, sparks flew. Josh knocked the rocks together like a madman, until, just as the sun set, the thread caught fire. Thirty-seconds later, a glow radiated from the depths of the wood, and in five minutes, the whole thing was up in smoke. Josh saved the rocks, and the others cheered at the light that was thrown against the dark ground and shadowy underbrush. Josh could not imagine them getting this far without having found the clearing. *Thanks, Ace,* he thought.

Josh retrieved the sharpened rock from Willam, and took two fish from the pool. He sliced them open along their bellies, cleaned out their innards, and stuffed some berries in them. He placed them on a rock very close to the heart of the fire. Ten minutes later, he turned the fish. They were cooking beautifully. Another ten minutes, and Josh removed the fish, cutting out five parts and distributing them. He woke Cory up and forced him to eat. He might be a killer, but he deserved to die happy, he *was* helping them survive...

Eating the fish was nasty business. Josh had to pick out the bones, skin and such with his fingers, revealing a disappointing amount of edible flesh. Josh threw the remnants into the river, the berries gave the fish a nice fresh taste. It was rather delicious, in fact. After dinner, Josh allowed each of them to take a handful of berries for dessert. Josh thoroughly enjoyed the sweet taste. The men retired to bed early, curling up on the hard ground under the tarp. Josh added enough wood to the fire to keep it running through the night. They slipped into unconsciousness almost instantly.

Josh was awoken by a loud growl. He looked up into the glowing eyes of a coyote. Josh slowly stood, the animal was back on it's hind legs, ready to pounce. Nobody else had woken. The beast growled again, and jumped. Josh reeled back out into the clearing. The animal circled Josh slowly, then pounced again. It hit Josh straight on this time. He toppled to the ground, feet from the fire. The coyote was on top of him. Josh reached a hand up and shoved it into the animal's mangy neck, keeping it barely from snapping the flesh off his face.

Josh reached out, his fingers scraping the edge of the knife stone, centimeters from his grasp. The animal surged suddenly against Josh, breaking past his arm. Josh rolled slightly to the side, the beast's teeth digging into the ground. Josh grabbed hold of the rock, bringing it over quickly, plunging the knife into the animal's neck. It sprawled to the side, yelping in pain. Josh rolled to his feet, grabbing one of the torches and shoving it into the fire. He swung it at the Coyote, keeping it at bay. Suddenly the beast turned and ran. Josh chased after it, leapt, and came down upon it, smashing the torch into it's skull.

The animal fell. Josh slit it's throat, just to be safe. He dragged it back to the fire and pulled it up onto the rocks, near the flames. It would slowly cook overnight. Josh fed more wood on the fire then cautiously went back to sleep, one eye open.

Josh and Alex awoke before the others, eating a handful of berries before heading down to the river, washing their faces to wake themselves up. The fire had continued to burn through the night, Josh added more wood. He was worried that he might not replicate the sparks of the night before. Josh set Alex to work picking more berries while he went into the woods to retrieve more fuel.

The others woke hours after, Josh and Alex had not stopped working, but they were glad the others had had good rest. They moved the coyote closer to the fire, they would eat it that night for dinner. They enjoyed a "hearty" breakfast of berries, and had three more of the fish for lunch. Josh set to work collecting wood all day, Cory picking berries, Willam catching fish, and Spencer tightening the ropes of the tarp and cleaned up the rest of the camp. Alex had the most interesting job of all.

Alex examined the berry bush and noticed some berries had been picked from the opposite side of the shrub. He knelt down and smelt the ground. Deer urine. He looked up to see a slightly defined path through the woods. He took the new device, the sharpened rock tied to a long stick, and headed into the brush. He followed the trail for some time before his ears picked up a faint noise. He hid himself in the thickets. The young deer trotted along the path, heading for some lunch. Alex let it pass then sprung from the bush, hurling the spear with all his might. It impaled straight through the deer's neck, killing it instantly.

Alex ran up and pulled the spear out, hoisting the animal over his shoulder and heading back to camp. The others cheered and clapped. They now had enough food to last the week. Josh looked at the camp and realized how far they had come. They might be able to breeze through the next couple days, and get out healthy. Josh was slightly worried about predators, he would instigate a night watch. Other than wood, they had enough supplies to last them the rest of the week. Josh was just glad they had found the place, the river was a massive asset.

Josh told the rest of the group to focus on collecting wood. By the end of the day, they had an enormous pile that towered above Josh's head. They were good for quite a while. On the end of the third night, Josh, Spencer, and Cory sat up around the fire, the last ones awake. The stars were startlingly brilliant out in the wilderness, Josh could even make out a strand of cosmic dust.

"That's where the facility is..." Cory said suddenly, pointing toward a dark space in the stars.

"How do you know?" Josh asked.

"Notice that the stars get dimmer toward that spot? It's not a cloud, it's light pollution," Cory explained. Josh had sat next to him that day at the berry bush, getting to know the man. He had had a very interesting childhood, with absentee parents, raised on movies and television. He had Aspergers syndrome, and had hours and hours of treatment as a child. He had mellowed out in the later years. Really, from the stories, Josh began to doubt that he was the killer. What if the murderer had been stabbed in the riot? Perhaps the deaths since then actually were suicides...

"Well, I'm going to hit the hay," Spencer announced, standing and moving to the tarp, snapping Josh's attention back to earth. He followed him, placing Cory in his hammock and adding more wood to the fire. The fourth day went by without a problem. Then the fourth night came.

Willam was awake on watch, his hand clenched around the thing in his pocket. It had taken a lot of work to get it there, but it would all be worth it soon. He pulled the item out of his pocket, examining it. Soon it would be time. *Now*, in fact. He would take action now. *Get it over with then disappear into the bush.*

Cory stirred in his hammock, slowly opening his eyes. He saw Willam standing in the clearing, the light of the fire reflecting off an object in his hand. Willam turned, making his way back toward the tarp. As he passed Cory, Cory realized what he was holding.

"Wake up! Willam's got a *gun!*" Cory was silenced when Willam smashed a hand down onto the man's throat, choking him. Josh sprung to his feet, in a combative stance. Alex and Spencer jumped up as well. Willam pulled Cory from the hammock and threw him down onto the ground. The splint snapped off his leg, splinters burying into his flesh. Cory screamed. Willam cocked the gun, leveling it at Cory. He pulled the trigger as Josh smashed into his side, knocking him to the ground. The bullet buried in the dirt. Willam scrambled to his feet, raising the gun at Josh.

"I was going to save you for last..." He spat, blood from his missing tooth streaming into his mouth. Josh was sweating, he knew he was about to get shot. Suddenly Alex came out of nowhere, smashing his shoulder into Willam, who stumbled back, tripping over the rocks and falling into the fire, which extinguished. Willam stood, cinders clung brightly on his exposed forearm, he showed no pain. It was then that Josh realized... Willam was completely insane.

Willam stepped out of the fireplace, brushing the cinders off his arm and sleeve. Some of his flesh was bubbling and bursting, he ignored the blistering burns. He raised his gun, Alex, Josh, and Spencer were standing in front of Cory, nobody could get at him now.

"I suggest you run, boys..." Willam smirked, "I've waited a long time to kill you three, your friendship kept me perfectly incognito to the rest of the camp. Yes, I've payed off the guards and The General, but they never knew who I was. I enjoyed my mind games with you, Josh..." Willam smirked, cocking the revolver once again. Josh recognized it as *his own gun.*

I don't want to get shot with my own gun, Josh recalled his conversation with Alexis, it felt like years ago... Josh knew that standing there was futile. He turned and sprinted back into the bush, in the direction Cory had labeled as the camp one night before. Willam stepped over Cory as he writhed on the ground, clutching at his leg. He stared down at him.

"You don't *belong* here. I've done a lot of work to get just me and those three in the woods here. You *deserve* this..." Willam smirked, lowering the gun at Cory. He pulled the trigger once, a bullet flying and piercing Cory's chest. Cory screamed out, his pain mixing with the echo of the gunshot. It had missed his vitals. Willam fired another shot, then another, and another. Cory's mutilated body stopped twitching, his own blood covered his dead face, specks of it had flung onto Willam's face. He licked his lips, enjoying the taste of his victims blood. He slowly limped off into the forest. He had severed a tendon on the back of his left leg when he fell into the fire, yet he still limped quickly, in his state of psychosis he felt no pain.

Josh heard the six gunshots and cringed, clearly envisioning the dead body on the ground. And that's when it clicked. Cory couldn't have been the killer...because of *that.* Cory was *there*, watching the basketball game, after Josh got out of the hospital, *during the second murder*. He couldn't have killed Chris. Suddenly all the pieces clicked together and lead Josh straight to... *Willam*. Josh's arm burned were Willam had bitten him on the second day. He was never rehabilitated in solitary, it had given him time to plan. Willam had to look insane in the beginning, then make his way into Josh's fold, so that any strange behavior could be explained. The plan was pure genius, and terrifying. Willam must have somehow had prior knowledge about Josh, or else how would he have known on the second day to get on his good side... and why?

"Joshua..." Willam called in a sing-song voice from somewhere in the forest, "Come out and play!" Willam fired a shot into the air, Josh instinctively ducked. Alex was running beside him, jumping logs and ducking branches. Josh knew that they couldn't run forever, they had to hide. They would never find their way back to the clearing, it was a matter of honor now, die at the hands of a psychopath or die at the hands of nature. Josh would not let Willam take another victim.

Josh pulled Alex down a hill, sliding under a fallen log that crossed a small dip. They lay there, uncomfortably cramped under the log, packed tightly together. Josh pulled a piece of bark over the entrance, blocking the view from where Willam would inevitably appear. Spencer ran down the hill as well, passing straight by the log and jumping into a thicket of brambles.

Willam came to the top of the hill, the cold steel heavy in the palm of his hand. He examined the mud streaks at the top of the hill, and made his way between the trees down the slope. Josh's breath was heavy, clinging to the suddenly cold air. Josh felt Alex breathing down his neck, his heart racing. Josh's vision was blurring white with adrenaline, tunneling down to view nothing but Willam making his way down toward them. He held his breath, not wanting to make the faintest noise. Willam's boot came directly in front of the log, and stopped.

"You were a very worthy adversary, Josh," Willam spoke. Josh felt as if he was talking directly to him, even if he didn't know where he was. Willam slowly reloaded the gun as he talked, clicking back the hammer. "I thought you almost had me in that riot business, I'll admit that it was a tactical error, but there were just too many to kill, too many better than me..." Willam angered himself with this, firing a shot into the wood. Josh was sure it was just out of anger, but it still startled him.

"I orchestrated the Mizuki situation... a failsafe to send you both to solitary should I need time to cover my tracks... it worked damn well too. Sorry I couldn't let you have her Josh, but you didn't have enough dirt on Alex. I studied you that first day, Josh, and learned every move you would make the entire rest of the year... what power I have, I must be God!" Willam shouted, firing three shots into the air. "Look at that, three shots left, one for each of you!" Willam's boot moved out of view. Josh silently shifted his weight, looking down the hill, watching Willam limp slowly on his injured leg.

He moved toward the bush where Spencer was hiding, and Josh caught his breath. Josh clambered over Alex, slowly sliding from under the log and standing to face his enemy. He had survived so much unbelievable shit at camp, he was sure he could face the maniac and live.

"What do you think of me now, *Dad*?" Willam screamed at nobody as he neared the bush, "Is my brother still better than me? *Is he*? I'm top of my class, *Dad*! Look at *me* now!" Willam came to a stop in front of the bush, taking a deep breath. "I can smell your fear, your sweat is sweet, Spencer..." Willam ripped half the bush out of the ground, tossing it aside. Josh tensed his legs, ready to sprint if the situation turned unsavory. Willam took Spencer by the collar and lifted him up, his feet dangling off the ground.

"You were a nuisance in the plan... I had expected a friendship between Alex and Josh, Alex would keep him busy enough to stay out of my business, thats why I had them bunk together! You were a *nuisance*, constantly distracting him from being distracted! You think all those little situations we got into were out of *friendship*? NO! They were to let Josh and Alex bond!" Willam threw Spencer to the ground, he fell to his knees. Willam pushed the barrel of the revolver into Spencer's forehead, drawing blood with the muzzle. Spencer closed his eyes, muttering a quick prayer. "God can't save you now, for he's the one *holding the gun!*" Willam yelled. Spencer shook with fear. Josh slowly began to make his way toward Spencer.

"Stand still, Josh, or I will pull the trigger now..." Willam announced without even turning around. Josh froze, Alex ten feet behind him. Sweat poured off his brow. "Spencer, I hereby pronounce you... *freed*," Willam pulled the trigger. Josh screamed. The hammer of the weapon smashed into the body of the gun, the bullet flew down the barrel, erupting out of the end of the pistol, ripping through Spencer's skin, smashing through his skull, and tore through his brain. The bullet passed through the other side of Spencer's head, taking a good amount of blood, skin, bone and grey matter with it. It painted the bush behind it red. Willam smirked, licking the end of the gun as he turned to face Josh. Spencer's body slumped to the ground.

Josh and Alex were shoulder to shoulder, ready for a fight. They would both break to opposite sides should fire commence. When Willam came to a full turn, Josh could see the fire burning in his eyes, he was looking into the depths of hell, straight at pure evil. Spencer's blood dripped from Willam's mouth, blending with his own.

"Now, Josh, the time has come. Your time, has come. I've been waiting all year for this. After I kill you, I will be top of my class... and finally make my parents proud. Alex, I will kill you after him, just to clean up loose ends. But I must complete my goal, before something goes wrong..." Willam pulled back the hammer and raised the pistol, pointing it straight at Josh's head. His hand did not shake. Josh saw no way out of the situation, but could stay alive slightly longer.

"Why, Willam? Why not actually try in your classes? Why go through all this to impress your Dad? Top of your class... is it really worth it?" Josh asked, fear wiped from his voice.

"Because... because... I'm not good enough..." Willam whispered to himself. Suddenly the rage burst forth, he screamed at Josh: "I'm not good enough, Dad! Don't you see? You never wanted me! You saw me as one of your *failed lab experiments*! How could you do that to me? I just want your love, Dad!" Willam yelled. Josh suddenly realized what it was... Willam had convinced himself that Josh was his father. Josh tried one last ditch effort to save his life.

"Willam, son, I'm proud of you. Good job, orchestrating all this, now, put down the gun, I'm proud of you..." Josh said in a very calm, loving voice. Willam lowered the gun slightly, sadness marked his face. Suddenly his face contorted into a look of sheer torture.

"Ahhhhhh!" He screamed at Josh, raising the gun again. He pulled the trigger, Josh closed his eyes and let the metal come at him. He heard the bullet hit skin, a grunt, then a thud. Josh heard Willam scream in anger, Josh opened one eye. Alex was sprawled on the ground in front of Josh, his shoulder bleeding profusely. Josh realized what had happened, Alex had jumped in front of him, taking the bullet for him. Josh was about to lean down to assist his friend, when willam raised his voice again.

"I won't miss this time, Josh!" Willam yelled, leveling the weapon.

"Neither will I!" A triumphant voice called from somewhere in the sky. Josh recognized it, but assumed he must be hearing things. Suddenly a brilliant spotlight lit up Willam from above. The lights in the helicopter came on, revealing the silent machine hovering several feet above Willam's head. The wind beat down on him, Ace sat on a jump seat mounted to the side of the chopper, shouldering a sniper rifle. Josh grinned up at his old friend, he had kept his promise. Willam turned and squinted up into the light, lowering his revolver.

"Willam H. Blackburn II, put the gun on the ground, and drop to your knees!" Ace called from the chopper. Willam squinted up into the light, looked back at Josh, then made a decision. He raised the pistol, first aiming it at Josh's chest. Ace pulled the bolt on the sniper rifle. Willam pulled back the hammer, pushing the barrel into his own chin, and pulled the trigger.

The bullet burst out the end of the barrel, cracking through Willam's lower jaw, ripping through the bone in the top of his mouth, and broke through to the left of his nose in a brilliant aerosol mist of shimmering blood. Willam rag-dolled to the ground, alive but limp. Two guards descended to the scene via cables from above. One knelt down and placed handcuffs around Willam's wrists, the second guard came up to Josh.

"You've been through a lot, you can come back early..." The guard said. Josh nodded slowly, pupils dilated at the sight of the attempted suicide. He helped the guard to carry Alex's body to the helicopter, and the five men ascended the ropes. They climbed into the body of the chopper and the door slid shut, the chopper veered away. Josh sat in the back of the chopper, Alex laying across the seats next to him, his head in his lap. Josh took off his shirt and held it against Alex's wound.

Ace and The General sat across from Josh, along with two guards. Willam's restrained body twitched on the ground. He had blown his entire lower jaw off, and ripped his nose out of it's place, but he was alive, bloody, but alive. The chopper flew, speeding toward the camp. They sat there in awkward silence, Willam moaned lightly, blood bubbling in his wounds.

"Josh," Ace broke the silence. Josh looked up from Alex's pained face, "My word is stone... I will protect you throughout your life."

"I know, Ace... Thank you," Josh replied, placing a hand on Alex's forehead.

"Josh, I'm sorry for not paying more attention to these murders... the pay was just too good..." The General said.

"Wait, pay?" Ace asked. The General began to sweat, "Were you payed to ignore the murders?"

"Yes, but... it was to keep panic from the inmates, er, students!" The General exclaimed.

"Brother," Ace said, "I think this will be your last year as administrator here." Josh smiled, both foes had fallen. The rest of the helicopter ride to the camp was uneventful. Apparently news of the attack had spread to the camp, for when the helicopter landed and Ace escorted Josh out, the rest of the students cheered at them. Josh assisted in taking Alex to the medical transport that was humming in the driveway. Ace got in the passenger seat, The General stayed at the camp. Josh hesitated before getting into the van. He watched a bleeding, limp Willam get loaded into the back of a heavily armored truck, Josh felt closure as the massive steel doors slammed shut and the multitude of locks were engaged. Josh climbed into the truck as the armored van pulled away.

"Ace, what'll happen to Willam?" Josh asked.

"He's going to spend the rest of his life in a nice little padded room, far out on an island that the company owns. He'll never get out of there," Ace replied from the front seat. Josh looked over at Alex on the stretcher next to him, and thought back of all the memories they had shared with Willam, and Josh realized the corrupted, calculating purpose behind each one. They watched the camp dissolve into darkness behind them. In seconds they were slowing to a stop in front of a tall, electronically lit building. Josh escorted

Alex to the medical ward, where he was closed out of the emergency room. Ace stood by him him in the elevator, to the fifteenth floor. Josh found his room and entered. It looked like a true hotel.

There was a queen sized memory foam bed, a large window overlooking a lake, a flat screen television, a large bathroom, a walk in closet, and a desk. Josh thanked Ace for saving him, making plans for lunch the next day. Josh shut the door and locked it. He drew the blinds, and disrobed. He flicked on the television before stepping into a hot shower. He washed the blood and dirt off himself, and tenderly massaged his wounds. He dried himself and found silk pajamas in his closet.

Josh slipped into the comfortable bed, the feathery mattress caressing him, it was the most comfortable he had been in a year. He managed ten minutes of Saturday Night Live before he careened off into deep sleep.

CHAPTER THIRTEEN

Josh awoke, the light from the blinds gently drifting through the room. He sat up, his wounds on fire, the rest of his body comfortably numb. Alex was sitting at the desk, eyeing the bacon on the breakfast platter that had been delivered while he slept. He wore blue medical robes and a white sling on his arm.

"Morning Josh. Better take this from me before I have any more, Ace already gave me a piece of his..." Alex smiled, awkwardly handing the tray to Josh with his left hand.

"Thanks, Alex," Josh mumbled, his voice hoarse from sleep. He placed the tray on his lap. He savored the bacon, it was only the second he had had in a year. The news was on, it was one week to the day Josh had left the orphanage, and there had been a chemical bomb scare in Vancouver, apparently it was all cleared up. Josh ate two pieces of toast, three eggs, four pieces of ham, five strips of bacon, a bowl of cereal, and three chunks of watermelon. He was ravenous after the time in the forest. The two sat in awkward, comfortable silence while the headlines streamed by. After a while, Alex spoke up.

"So, it was Willam all along..." Alex said, Josh didn't want to discuss the topic.

"You took a bullet for me, Alex. Why?" Josh asked.

"Well, you're my best friend, but... there was something else. I failed every test I took after I got back from solitary... I wasn't in the passing grade. I'm going back to prison. At the time, I wanted that shot to kill me. But now, seeing you here, in specialty housing, I'm glad I survived. But if it was either of us, I deserved it. I'm an outlaw, you have more right to live."

"That's not true. We both have an equal right to live. I'm glad you survived too," Josh smiled back at his friend. He took a long sip of the tea on the table next to him, "God, I forgot what a quality cup of Earl Grey tasted like."

Alex left a short time after, Josh soaked in a warm bath for an hour, then descended upon the closet. He dressed himself in a pair of comfortable jeans, a tee shirt, a checkered over shirt, hanging open, and a casual blazer. Josh brushed his teeth. He went out the doorway and to the bottom floor. There was a cavernous room with pool tables, poker tables, and televisions. Josh recognized several men from the camp playing, chatting, and laughing. If the camp was purgatory, this was heaven. Josh left the building and went around the back, walking the long path around the lake, pondering those who had died, and why he had survived. There must be a reason. Josh met Ace for lunch later that day, sitting down in the elegant restaurant on the third floor.

"Enjoying your room, Josh?" Ace asked.

"You have no idea..." Josh smiled, "So, The General is no longer in power?"

"Yes, you can just call him Bruce now. He won't be terrorizing students anymore. I've reassigned him to the head of the specialty guard in the facility that Willam is being kept at," Ace replied. It seemed to Josh that something was troubling Ace.

"Seems like a job that would fit him..." Josh laughed. He sipped his soda, a heaping burger arrived, it truly was heaven. They had casual conversation until at the end of the meal when Josh finally brought up the subject pressing his mind.

"What's going to happen to Alex?" Josh asked. Ace exhaled heavily, leaning back in his chair.

"He failed his exams, but he is here... He survived that business in the woods, and took a bullet for a friend, with his sniping skills taken into consideration, I may be able to pull some strings. He'll have to go back to the prison for now, everybody must go back to where they came from... but I may be able to get him a lower ranking job at the agency..." Ace answered. Josh smiled, happy at the news. Josh stood to go but Ace pulled him back.

"Josh, I need to tell you something about Willam..." Ace said. Josh sat, emotions mixed at the name.

"What?" Josh asked.

"You had told me that Willam said his motivation was to impress his father... Willam doesn't have a father, Josh. He was produced in a laboratory, a *failed experiment*. He seemed to operate functionally in society, so they let him live. But there was never anybody he could have mistaken for a father," Ace explained. Josh pondered this. How deep was Willam's psychosis?

The two parted ways, Ace heading off to some administrative business, and Josh back to his room, to catch up on the world's news that had passed while he was in camp. Later that day, Alex stopped by Josh's room.

"Hey, Josh, you hear the announcement?" Alex asked. Josh stood up, not having heard it, "The camp's award ceremony will take place in two days. I don't suppose I'll be winning anything, but you're top of the class, I think that you will need to attend..." Alex laughed. Josh nodded, his mind on the fritz, calculating all the political ramifications from the news of the year.

"Yeah, I'll be there..." Josh replied.

"Its at one PM, and they say you should wear the tuxedo in your closet, with your formal combat jacket hanging open over it," Alex explained. Josh thanked him and sent him on his way. Josh suddenly had a plan of how to get Alex into the I.E.M.F. for sure. Josh smirked as the door shut behind Alex, snickering with his plan. Later that day he checked in at the hospital ward, where they looked at his various wounds, applied some bandages, and sent him on his way. Josh retired to his room. The next day was spent much the same, re-hashing events with other inmates, and a full debriefing with Ace. And then the ceremony day came.

*   *   *

Josh looked sharp in his tuxedo, the bow tie he had so meticulously straightened. He pulled his military jacket over it, it was still stained with Alex's blood. Josh did up the bottom three buttons, making it look more uniform. He took a deep breath, not sure he could face the two coffins that would be undoubtedly be attending as well.

Josh waited in the elevator, alone. He stepped out and was met by Ace, who placed a long, crimson sash across his chest.

"Josh, you're the valedictorian. Ready to get out there and rejoin the world?" Ace asked.

"I... I think so," Josh replied, nervous. His plan was coming together. He pushed through the backdoors of the building, out toward the lake. On the bank was a beautiful stage, crafted of a dark wood. It was raised three feet off the ground, a sea of seats in front of it. The students mulled about, ecstatic. Josh recognized the slightly different faces of several older men and women, parents and siblings. Josh felt alone, but then he realized, every man there was his family.

Ace led Josh up onto the stage, sitting down beside him, he was the only student on the stage. The General and The Master were there, as well as two top guards and a man that Josh didn't recognize.

"That man's name is Sheldon, he's the head of the I.E.M.F. One of my best friends, quite the man. Takes an amazing mind to get all that in order. I really admire him," Ace whispered to Josh, who had never heard him speak so highly of anyone before. The other men on the stage sat as well, except The General, who stood behind the podium. The men and women in the audience took their seats as well.

"Ladies and Gentlemen, soldiers and students, please stand," The General called. Josh glanced at the two mahogany coffins that where positioned between the stage and the audience, imagining the mutilated remains of Cory and Spencer laying there. Over Spencer's coffin, a draped British flag. Over Cory's coffin, a Canadian flag. Josh truly didn't know what flag his own coffin would have bore.

Suddenly a lone trumpet broke the silence, giving a sad, lonely call out across the lake. The beautiful song lasted two minutes, then fell silent. The students and officials saluted, the guests placed their hands over their hearts. In the full minute of silence, a single tear ran down Josh's cheek, memories of Spencer streamed through his head. The General stepped up to the podium, clearing his throat.

"Thank you for the moment of silence for those who have passed naturally at the facility, along with the devastating series of murders that racked the camp. We would like to say that the man responsible has been clinically diagnosed as psychopathic, and is now in our captivity. In the long months that these fine young men and women have endured, I have personally watched them mature, harden, and become stronger people. I don't want to drag this out, I know you all are positively ecstatic to get home after a year away, and I don't feel that a speech from some faceless official will do you much justice. So here, to give the one and only speech that will be given in this ceremony, your valedictorian, Joshua Stone," The General finished. There was much applause. Ace clapped Josh on the shoulder as he stood to approach the podium.

"Hello," He paused for the applause to finish, "Actually, I don't think that I am fit to give this speech. Sure, I had the highest grade, but personally, and I believe it is the collective opinion here, that there is a student out there much more fit to give this speech. That man, who took a bullet for me, literally. So here is your valedictorian, Alex Whittemore," Josh announced in a clear, steady voice. Alex had a look of stunned surprise on his face. He stood slowly, making his way toward the stage. When he came up to the podium, Josh removed his sash and placed it around Alex. The man looked like a true veteran, in his formal dress and the white sling on his arm. He cleared his voice and leaned his head forward toward the mic. Josh expected him to be nervous and taken by surprise, but Alex began his speech like a true hero.

"Let us not be too overwhelmed in the celebratory nature of this event. In the casket in front of you lay one of the best friends I've ever had, Spencer Eberstark. He will be missed. But, we *must* push forward. We must *move on*. The men and women seated here are the best of the best. I served time in prison before this, and if I had not, I would not have survived, hell, I barely did anyway. This camp was no free ride, let me tell you that. And I realize that not everybody can get through, but in my mind, we have all surmounted something far more impressive than the most educated professionals in society.

"I have seen more blood, hate, terror and pure humanity here, than anywhere in my life. The men and women I see in front of me today, even if I have not spoken to them personally, I feel a sort of brother-ship toward. God, I'm really bad at giving speeches, aren't I? Wow, you know what? I've never really found the point of these closing speeches. You've all lived through this... you don't need my stories to remind you of that. Anybody out there who needs to know, will hear it from you. So, I'm going to step down now, and let you all go back to your families and homes. Thank you,"

Alex finished his speech, the students cheered and clapped. Alex was instructed to take a seat next to Josh. The General stepped forward, and listed off the top ten percent of the grade.

"Those men and women will begin their promising careers at the I.E.M.F. The rest of you, I apologize, but you just aren't made of the right stuff. We will assure you promising roles in the highest places of global government, law, medicine, or whatever path you choose to follow. Of those men and women I just listed, some thirty, ten will be chosen as the best of the best... the agents of the I.E.M.F. These men and women have climbed the ladder... and reached the top. Honorary agency will be awarded to the two brave souls that lay before you, killed in the horrible slaughter in the forest," The General called out. As he did, the two high guards on the stage stepped down, saluted the coffins, and placed two small, golden medals with a red feathered cross and a blue bird emblazoned on them. The guards returned to the stage, saluting the caskets once again. Josh had a difficult time suppressing tears, he could clearly see Spencer standing on the stage, the medal on his chest.

"Now, the ten men and women who have come out on top... Joshua Stone... Edward..." The rest of the list was blurred out to Josh. He stood, shaking first The General's hand, then The Masters's hand, then finally Sheldon's hand. Ace pinned the metal to Josh's military jacket, smiling at his pupil. Josh stood at the end of the stage, joined by eight other students. There was an odd pause before the tenth agent was announced.

"Now, this tenth man, I think, has truly earned the title I.E.M.F. agent," Ace spoke clearly into the mic, "He survived the forest massacre, took a bullet for a friend, and is the best damn survivalist I have ever seen. He may not be the most book smart of them, but he is definitely the most street smart. So now, for the first time in the history of camp Razor's Edge, a man who did not make the top ten percent becomes an agent. Alex Whittemore, get up here!" Ace called. Josh clapped, bursting with joy. Alex joyously shook the men's hands and accepted his medal gleefully. He bounced along the stage, taking his place beside Josh. The two men hugged, amazed at the turn of events.

"The men and women you see up here on this stage have come as far as they can with us, and now they set out on a new adventure... Welcome to the agency..." Sheldon announced from the podium. The crowd went wild, applauding and cheering. Alex and Josh looked at each other from the corner of their eyes, amazed they had survived... they had come so far...

"The men and women here will spend two months in their respective homes around the world, then leave again for their mandatory year of military service," Sheldon announced. Josh's hearing tunneled. He and Alex slowly turned their heads to look at each other, then snapped their attention back to the podium, yelling in unison:

"What?!!"

EPILOGUE

    A bus, the same bus that Josh had taken to the camp one year ago, slowly pulled to a stop. Alex stood before the location was announced, he knew where they were. Josh looked up at him, knowing that he had to face his past.

    "Kent institution," The bus driver called. Alex walked slowly down the aisle, the men and women in the seats staring up at him. He came to the doorway and slowly turned back to face Josh. He raised a hand in farewell. Alex turned and walked out the door, immediately flanked by two guards. Josh suddenly stood, sprinting down the aisle, grabbing the doors just as they closed, forcing them back open. Alex turned to look back.

    "Alex, come to the head quarters with me. I'll work it out with Ace, you don't need to return here..." Josh begged.

    "I'm sorry Josh, but I need to face my past. I cannot willingly step out into the field before all past conflicts are resolved, all the hatchets buried. I might get beaten, spat upon, maybe even attacked, but I will stay alive. I won't try to escape, that might cost me the agency, but for you Josh, I swear I will survive. I'll see you at the air base in two months. Have a nice break," Alex replied, valiantly. With that he turned and walked into the front doors of the prison, more free than he had been when he left.

Josh checked his emotions, turning back into the bus, taking his seat again. Three hours later, he was one of two left on the bus. They pulled into a vast parking garage, the bus was unloaded. Josh heaved his backpack onto his shoulder, stuffed with memories, and hefted the guitar out of the back. The two men that stood in the parking garage nodded goodbye as the empty bus pulled away. Josh noticed that the man standing next to him wore an Agent's badge on his chest.

"Hello, I'm Joshua Stone, agent..." Josh said, extending his hand to the man.

"My name's George, nice to meet you!" The man replied, shaking Josh's hand. The next two hours rushed by for Josh. There was an interview, thousands of forms and documents, pictures, identification cards, and introductions. Finally, Josh was standing in front of a brilliant mahogany door, Ace beside him.

"This has been officially designated as your flat, Josh..." Ace explained. He handed Josh a keycard. Josh cautiously slid it through the lock, the door clicked open. Josh pushed through and was met by a beautiful room. It had eggshell white walls, a long hallway that led from the front door. There was a small guest bedroom off to the left with a bathroom, a sizable master bedroom on the right with a huge bathroom and walk in closet. The hall emptied into a gigantic living room with a vaulted ceiling, a marble laden bar stood in the back, a door led to a kitchen and an office. A floor to ceiling window ran along the back wall, overlooking the city, Josh stared out amazed, the bustling people in the streets below, the cars and vendors... it was all so much. Josh had never seen a city before, even though he had lived in that very building his entire life.

"Ah, Vancouver..." Ace sighed. Josh set his backpack down in the center of the living room, took a few seconds to look around the room, then turned to Ace.

"This place needs a few lava lamps..." Josh stated. Ace chuckled.

"I'll take you to Ikea in a week... then to the DMV, I can't drive you around forever..." Ace laughed. Some time later, Josh found himself sitting in the interestingly decorated office of Sheldon. It seemed like a clash between a hunting cabin, a hippie's bedroom, and a state of the art office. Josh sat nervously in front of the desk, not knowing what news the big boss would bring. Sheldon pushed through the beads that hung in front of a long hallway, taking a seat behind his desk. leaning back, placing his feet on the desk. He threw a piece of gum into his mouth, and began to chew. Josh felt he would become very good friends with the man.

"Josh, I know you still need to serve your military time before you become a true agent here, but I think I will send you out into the field twice over the next two months, wouldn't want you to get bored..." The man smirked, Josh nodded, "You see, there are three levels of agent here at the I.E.M.F. Agents, Full Agents, and O.P.P. Five men make up O.P.P, and are so elite, you will probably never meet the other four. Full Agents are regular agents that have successfully served at least five years at the agency, and must meet a few other requirements. In the first three years of your work here at the I.E.M.F, you will need a Full Agent as a partner. Don't think you're an exception to this. You will have a partner for the next two months, as well as the three years after you return... and he's standing outside right now." Sheldon pressed a button and the heavy, automatic door to the office slid open.

Josh looked around the side of the chair, and was surprised at the man standing there. Sudden joy overwhelmed him. His new partner entered the room, sat beside Josh, and addressed Sheldon:

"Sir, what's our mission?" Ace asked.

*   *   *

The small cell held the bulky man in dangerously tight quarters. It had been one year since the bus crash after graduation, and the man who swept him away. He remembered his childhood friend, and wondered if he had gotten out of the camp alive. He thought of the year he had been trapped there, and wondered when he would be released. Suddenly the door creaked open, the light blinded the man. The door closed, the prisoner recognized the man standing before him... he had been there the day he was taken...

"Hello, Mason," The captor smirked, "I have an interesting career opportunity for you..."

*   *   *

The waves lapped up against the side of the rock and the cement building that stood atop it. The horrid conditions in the middle of the ocean wore away at the building, it would eventually crumble, taking the inmates with it. Inside, The General sent the guard out of the room, pushing the trolley down the hall. The lights above him flickered, and the screams of the insane blended with the crashing of the waves. The guard slowly pushed trolley down the hall, a single metal door stood at the end of the hall. The plate on it read '715'.

The guard cautiously approached the door, and slid away the grate at the eyehole, the animal inside was standing inches from the hole, staring straight out into space, as always. The guard was unsettled, the creature never addressed the guard. He never moved, never talked, never blinked. The guard took the tray of food off the trolley and shoved it through the hole, quickly sliding it shut, not wanting to see the beast anymore. Inside the room, the man shoved the food directly down his throat, he had no means of chewing it.

He finished his dinner and smiled, as much as you can with no bottom jaw and a massive hole in the side of your face. He retreated to the corner of the room, curling into a ball holding his knees against his chest. He smiled a deformed, crooked gash, grinning off into space. He clearly saw his enemy standing in the middle of the room, mocking him. The man let out a shrieking laugh, he took a deep breath but smelt nothing. He scratched at what was left of his nose, still shrieking and laughing. He stood, approaching the illusion standing in the middle of the small, white padded cell.

He came up to the man standing there, curiously investigating him. He was so lifelike, but why visit him now? He reached forward and punched the man in the face, the man who had cost him his jaw. Josh took the punch, smiled, and vanished into the wall of the room. The man ran after him, colliding into the concrete, falling back. He screamed, his scream slowly transforming into a laugh. He laughed like a hyena, uncontrollably.

"I'm coming for you, Josh..." Willam spit through his deformed, psychopathic grin. He chuckled, "I swear."

ABOUT THE AUTHOR

Tristan R.B. is a pen name. Tristan isn't even my first name. I live in Surrey, BC, Canada. I'm just an average kid, born in '98... I love paintball, (Go SAS!) writing, and traveling... not really much else to say. If you're reading this, you must have really enjoyed the book, usually I just skim over the about the author, so if you're reading this, good on 'ya. There will be sequels (and maybe prequels) to this book, so keep an eye out. Keep reading!
   -Tristan R.B.

Friends are divided.

Innocent blood is spilled.

A mentor will fall.

CPSIA information can be obtained at www.ICGtesting.com
Printed in the USA
LVOW05s1720270114

371154LV00038B/3392/P